WRANGLE ME, COWBOYS

Coyote Ranch
Book 2

Alexa B. James

Published in the United States by Alexa B. James and Speak Now.
Cover design by Ally Hastings at Starcrossed Covers

This edition:
ISBN-13: 978-1-945780-26-4

DEDICATION

For you, dear reader.

ONE

Amber

The day after I kissed my stepbrother, I woke up to the bright light of a Wyoming morning. The room was a bit chilly, but I snuggled down under the comforter and smiled to myself, remembering that kiss. Remembering the sensation of Holden's huge, muscular body pressing against mine. Remembering his cock hardening against me.

I rolled over and pulled open the drawer of the nightstand, reaching for my vibrator. I'd gotten used to being sexually frustrated after three years of dating a hold-out who turned out to be a cheating piece of shit—who was only holding out on me.

To my even greater frustration, as my hand brushed the bottom of the empty drawer, I realized I'd left my vibrator back in New York. After all, I'd thought I was coming here to babysit, not fall into paroxysms of lust over three sexy cowboys. With a groan, I fell back on my pillow, my arm across my eyes. What a craptastic way to ruin the good feeling I'd had when I woke.

On the nightstand, my phone buzzed, taunting me.

I picked it up and looked at it, an idea forming in my mind. My phone vibrated....

Five minutes later, I called my best friend Haley back. "I need an intervention," I blurted when she answered.

"Aww, Amber. Are you drinking yourself into a coma every night thinking of how much you miss me?"

"I do miss you," I said. "But no. I'm pretty sure I just violated my phone in ways no one has ever done before. I can't even believe I'm holding it against my face right now."

"Did you put it *inside* your underwear?" Haley asked.

"What? How did you even know what I was talking about?"

"Emergency vibe," she said, as if it were obvious.

I tried not to think about how many times I'd used her phone.

"So, did you?" she asked. "Because yeah, that's like sexual assault of a mobile device. But otherwise, you're good."

"Then I'm good," I said, relieved that I wasn't the first woman to get desperate enough to hump her iPhone.

"And hey, no pussy juice on your face," Haley added.

I couldn't help but laugh. "Did you just call it pussy juice?"

"Well, I could have said come, but you'd probably enjoy getting come on your face."

"You'd know."

"It's like a warm facial," she said. "But seriously, Am. Just go buy a vibrator."

"There are no cabs here," I said. "No buses. No subway. Basically, I'm trapped and at the mercy of my stepbrothers."

"Ahhh," she said. "So that's why you need to masturbate with your phone. The sexy stepbrother. Which one are you lusting after this time?"

"All of them," I wailed. "I can't decide. And honestly, Haley, I don't think they want me to."

"Don't tell me they're putting you in a nunnery like Cheating Charlie."

That was the name Haley had given my ex after we walked in on him having a threesome. For years, I'd let him know I'd be open to sex or other things, but he'd been insistent on preserving my virginity. Like it was something to put in a freaking museum.

"I'm not sure," I said. "They definitely aren't trying to shut me up in a nunnery, but are related..."

"Uh...no? To be related, they'd have to be your actual brothers."

"So you'd be cool sleeping with your stepbrothers?"

"Ew, no, because they're little kids, and I was there when they were born," Haley said. "You just met these guys. And if they want you and you want them... No judgment."

"But there's three of them. What if they get jealous and weird?"

"So they all want you, together, at the same time?"

"I think so," I squeaked.

"Well, I guess you won the breakup. A foursome beats a threesome."

"Four mouths are better than three," I said, paraphrasing the evil ex, and we both dissolved into laughter. But under the laughter, it still hurt. The sting of rejection hadn't quite worn off yet.

But I did wonder about my stepbrothers, which meant I was moving on. The question was, which one of them would I move on with? Holden had told me I didn't have to choose. Maybe he hadn't meant it the way I'd taken it. Maybe he'd meant it like, I didn't have to worry about choosing because they would never hook up with their stepsister, no matter how perfect that kiss had been.

But I didn't think so. I thought he meant it like, I didn't have to choose because I could have them all. Which just seemed too good to be true, and also, I worried about the logistics of it. Would I rotate from one room to the next each night? Would we need to make a schedule? What if I needed a night off or I had my period? What if one of them got mad because I made more noise in the room next door with his brother? What if I just wanted to be held by big, cuddly Holden, but it was rough-and-ready Waylon's night?

Or would it be a foursome—all three of them at the same time? And if it was that, could I handle it?

TWO

Amber

When I dragged myself out of bed at last, I did my usual morning routine at a leisurely pace—shower, get dressed, make myself a simple breakfast, and head out to take a walk. In the distance, I could see one of the tractors in the field, and a cowboy-hatted figure bending over the fence. The sun was bright on the thin layer of snow that had fallen—the first snow of the year.

I smiled as I approached the figure. I could tell by his massive barrel chest and towering treelike height that it was Holden, and that Sawyer was just beyond him, also working on the fence.

"Hey," I said, waving so they'd know I was nearby and not sneaking up on them to spy on their conversation. Which I kinda wanted to do, just to see if Holden had told Sawyer about kissing me yet.

"Howdy, Princess," Sawyer said, tipping his brown leather hat at me, dimples sinking into his tan cheeks.

I seriously wanted to kiss him, too.

God, I was terrible. But maybe understandable, considering what I'd recently been through.

"What are you up to?" Holden asked, smiling from beneath the brim of his hat. He was wearing what I'd begun to think of as "the ranch uniform." Canvas coveralls, work gloves, and boots.

"Just walking," I said with a shrug. "But I wouldn't mind learning to something useful around here. If I'm going to be here for three months, I might as well become...I don't know. A ranch hand?"

Sawyer laughed, the corners of his blue eye crinkling as he squinted up at me from where he was crouched, holding a strand of barbed wire taut with one gloved hand while he twisted the end with a pair of pliers. "You want to be a ranch hand?"

"Yeah, or something," I said. "So I'm not just sitting around the house looking pretty."

"But you do that so well."

"Shut up," I said. "I told you, I'm not here to be your Holly Housewife."

"Don't tell our ma that," Holden said. "That's the only reason she'd find acceptable for you being here."

"Wow, your dad better not be expecting that from my mom," I said. "She's pretty much married to her seat on the senate, and the only thing she knows how to make is a gin-and-tonic."

"Can't wait to meet her," Sawyer said. "She sounds lovely."

I laughed and shook a finger at him. "Don't insult my mother. Only I can do that."

"Ditto."

"If that was meant to distract me, it's not going to work," I said. "Come on, don't make me sit around inside all winter. I'll go nuts. In New York, there was a party pretty much every night of the week. Either at school, or a political dinner, or a photo opportunity for one of my parents that I had to attend, or a fundraiser, or a club opening..."

"That sounds...exhausting," Holden said. "I'm sorry."

I stared at him. "I think the word you're looking for is *exciting*."

"Oh," he said, ducking his head. "Sorry. I thought you were complaining."

"I'm complaining about not having anything to do," I said. "Seriously, guys. I'll get that cabin fever thing, like the guy in *The Shining*."

"We can't have that," Sawyer said seriously, but I could see the laughter glinting in his eyes as he stood and moved on to the next section of fence.

"I know, right?" I said, tagging along. "I mean, I don't even know what a boiler is, but if you have one, I'll definitely blow it up."

"Good thing Waylon's not out here," Sawyer said. "He'd hate to hear you threatening our ranch that way."

"Okay, I admit, Waylon has seen me make a few small missteps," I said. "But no one was hurt. And if you give me a job, what's the worst that could happen? It's not like I'm going to run around murdering all the cows, and that's how you make your living, right? And there's barely a tree on the ranch, so it's not like I can burn it down."

"Grass fires are a very dangerous thing," Holden said, frowning at me.

"Okay, I promise not to light any fires," I said, throwing up my hands. "And I'm not a cow-napper, so you don't need to worry about that. I just need something to do so I'm not sitting around thinking about my ex-boyfriend."

"What about the horses?" Sawyer asked Holden. "Grimes is getting on in years, and he's got a lot of other things to take care of."

"Sounds good," Holden said. "How are you with horses, Amber?"

I rolled my eyes and hid a grin. I should have started with the boyfriend thing. That got them looking for ways to distract me in a hurry. It was true, though. I hated thinking about Charlie, but when I had nothing else to do, sometimes I'd start sinking into despair at how many years I'd wasted on the bastard. But the distance had already given me perspective, and most of the time, I didn't even wish he'd fall onto the subway tracks and be crushed to death.

Mostly I just hoped he'd get a venereal disease

and his dick would slowly, painfully rot away to nothing.

But the real danger wasn't that I'd get depressed about why he hadn't loved me enough to sleep with me, though he'd been happy to stick it to a couple random chicks at the same time. The real danger was that sometimes, in my darkest moments, I wondered if he was thinking about me. Because as sick as it made me to admit, I'd honestly loved him. Or at least I'd loved the boy I knew.

But that boy wasn't Charlie. That boy was a pretty lie. Nothing we'd had was real, and if I took him back, I'd never be able to trust him again. And worse, I'd never be able to trust myself again. I'd fully bought into his whole act, which just proved I had zero lie-detecting skills and was a complete sucker.

"Amber?" Holden asked. "Have you ever ridden a horse?"

"Sorry," I said quickly. "See, thinking about my ex right now. You've got to help me."

"That asshole doesn't deserve a second of your thoughts," Sawyer said with a scowl.

"And to answer your question, I took riding lessons for a while. So yes, I know how to ride."

"Great," Sawyer said. "That's something you can do."

I could think of two things I'd like to do. They were standing right in front of me. But it didn't seem wise to say that out loud. I'd already freaked them out once. From now on, I was going to keep my head down, work on the ranch, and stay away from drama, the same way my stepbrothers did all day.

And maybe order a vibrator online to get me through the nights.

THREE

Holden

I was kind of nervous to teach Amber how to ride, but since I was the calmest, my brothers thought I would be the best choice. I wouldn't start yelling and spook the horses—not that Van Gogh would spook. I'd named all the horses after artists, back when I'd had the stable job. We'd passed it on to Grimes, but he was getting along in years and would probably like a decrease in responsibilities.

I showed Amber where the feed was, and how much to give them, and where to put it. "You'll want to feed and water them twice a day," I told her. "Here pretty soon, the water will freeze at night so you'll need to check and make sure the heating element is doing its job. If there's water, not ice, then they'll be fine. We'll bring them hay, so you just got to get them some feed. And then let them out so they can run and graze, when there's not too much snow on the ground." I showed her the door to let them out, and the field where they exercised, as well as the corral.

"What if they don't come back at night?"

"They will," I assured her. "If you're not sure about anything, you can always shout for one of us. And Grimes is usually nearby, so he can check in on you and make sure everything's going okay. He'll take care of the larger maintenance, like getting the farrier in to trim their hooves and check their shoes, and getting their medications. He can also keep up with mucking the stalls, unless you're just dying to throw horse shit."

Amber wrinkled her cute little nose. "I'm good, thanks."

"Don't worry," I said, squeezing her shoulder. She felt so slight under my big paws that I felt like an oaf touching her, like I was mauling her. "It's really pretty easy, once you get the hang of it. And you can throw some fresh bedding in after Grimes cleans the stalls, or let him do it. Now, you ready to meet them?"

"Definitely," Amber said, looking over at the stalls. Van Gogh had her head out and was watching us. The rest were still eating from their feeders.

"Looks like Van Gogh agrees with me," I said. "She's the gentlest, so you'll do fine on her."

I thought Amber might hold back, but she wasn't a bit afraid. She walked right up and held her hand out, letting Van Gogh mouth her palm. Finding nothing there, Van Gogh snorted. Amber laughed and stepped closer, running her hand up the horses cheeks and scratching her forehead while Van Gogh sniffed at her neck. I could tell they'd make fast friends, and my riding lessons wouldn't amount to more than one lesson.

"We'll take them out in a couple hours, after they've had time to digest," I said. "I'll show you a good trail to get some exercise on. The others will probably want to follow, but you don't have to take them. They'll get their exercise in the field."

By the time she'd loved on all the horses, and I'd shown her the blankets, how to check the horses over so if they were acting funny or had anything unusual going on, she'd be more likely to spot it, it had been over an hour. Amber wanted to brush them down, so we worked on that. I didn't figure a city girl would be interested in horses, but maybe it was because she'd never been around them. Maria had been scared of horses and wouldn't even ride unless one of us rode behind her. Now that I thought about it, that might have been just another part of her game.

Amber wasn't the sort who wanted to look helpless and scared, though. Sometimes she could be a little clueless, but I figured that was just the way she'd grown up. I couldn't expect her to know more about horses or tractors than I knew about the New York subway. It was something I'd seen on TV, that was all. Same with her.

When the horses got restless to go outside, I saddled up Van Gogh, showing Amber how to do it, too, but reminding her to ask Grimes for help if she wanted to ride when we weren't around. Then I saddled up Picasso and put leads on the other two so they could get some exercise before the snows got too deep to ride the trails.

"Ready?" I asked Amber. She strode over, patted Van Gogh, and stuck her foot in the stirrup. I guided her hand to the saddle, aware of the heat of her body so near mine. My cock stirred at the memory of our kiss the other night, and having my hand on her ass as I helped her into the saddle didn't help.

Damn, this was bad. We were supposed to be looking out for this party girl, not falling for her. But as we rode out, I couldn't stop. It had been way too long since I'd had a woman in my bed, that was all. I kept telling myself that, but it didn't stop me from seeing sexiness in everything Amber did. Her rhythm in the saddle, her thighs around the horse, her tight little ass in those designer jeans she wore—she had my cock straining against my jeans, wanting her riding me that way.

When the horses were warm and I thought she could handle it, I urged Picasso ahead, letting him run a little. Rembrandt and Frida cantered along beside us, used to this routine. Looking back over my shoulder, I saw Amber riding with her eyes closed, her head thrown back and her blonde hair flowing out in the wind behind her. God damn, she was beautiful.

Too beautiful for us to destroy her with our perversions. She looked so pure and joyful in that moment, not like the kind of woman who wanted to be plowed by three cowboys at once. Amber wasn't a girl to take turns fucking—she was one to treasure and care for. I'd floated the other idea by her, and she'd seemed interested, but she hadn't said yes. Now I could see that it would be a mistake. We were supposed to be getting to know this girl, not having an orgy with her.

She was part of our family now, a girl we should protect as we would our own sister. And that's what we were going to do. If not because she was our stepsister and that's what we'd been asked, then because she deserved it. And because I cared about her too much to ruin her the way we would if we let ourselves.

FOUR

Amber

The next morning, it was my very first day to feed and tend the horses on my own. They hadn't wasted any time giving me some responsibility. I'd thought they'd give me a week of training or something, but they seemed to trust that I could remember the right amount of feed and water.

Van Gogh whinnied when she saw me, swinging her head in my direction. The horses were already getting used to me, like Holden said they would, and soon they'd look forward to my visits, knowing that meant they were getting food.

When I turned to feed Picasso, Mr. Grimes was standing in the wide aisle that ran the length of the barn, between the stalls.

"Hi," I said, raising a hand to him. While I was distracted, Van Gogh reached out, grabbed the edge of the scoop, and dumped her oats all over the floor at my feet.

"You brat," I said, pushing her head away. I refilled the scoop and fed her, poured Picasso's oats in his feed pan, then turned back to the metal drums. I bent down to fill the scoop, and when I turned, Mr. Grimes was still standing there, leaning on the gate of one of the stalls, watching me.

Okay, that's a little creepy.

Ignoring him, I went about feeding the rest of the horses. He was probably just watching to make sure I did everything right. I was new, after all, and he'd been doing this for years. Still, it was unnerving to have him just stand there, not hovering but observing. When I finished, I brushed off my hands and blew the hair off my face.

"Did I pass?" I asked.

Mr. Grimes grunted.

"Well, then," I said. "I'll take that as a yes."

When he still didn't speak, I started to get a creeping feeling in my gut, so I headed for the door. Just as I passed him, I heard a single word uttered.

"Whore."

The word hit me like a bullet, hard and unforgiving. I stumbled before righting myself and turning to face him.

"Excuse me?"

"I know what you been up to in that house." His voice was gravelly and nasal, with a strong southern twang.

I took a step back. "What?"

"My wife told me all about it." His eyes crawled over me with a mixture of disgust and lust. "I know what kind of girl you is."

"You don't know anything about me," I said, forcing my voice to remain calm and steady. "And neither does your wife."

"I know you ain't got morals nor standards," he said. "Letting a group of men take turns with you." His lip curled into a sneer as his eyes roamed over my body.

"We don't *take turns* doing anything but making dinner," I said coldly. "And what your wife saw the other day was my brothers keeping me from dying of hypothermia. If she saw something dirty in that, maybe she's the one who needs to look at her morals."

With that, I whirled on my heels and stomped out of the barn, but not before I heard him mutter after me, "Jezebel."

The nerve of that guy! I was shaking with rage as I stomped back to the house. Here I was, taking over the horses to make his job easier, and he was calling me a whore. I had half a mind to go back out there and give him another lecture. But knowing me, I'd spill out way too much and it would come back to haunt me. After all, his wife was at least a little bit right about that night. It hadn't been completely innocent. Had it?

*

A while later, when I'd calmed down, I saw Waylon heading for the shop out beyond the five empty cabins behind the house. I threw together a sandwich as an excuse and let myself out the back door. I

19

wasn't sure if Holden had told his brothers about our kiss, or if I should tell them first. I didn't know how this whole thing worked at all, but I knew they didn't like secrets. If I came clean about it, I figured they'd respect me. Then again, it might get Holden in trouble.

Either way, I wanted to feel Waylon out, see how he felt about it and find out if he knew. So I balanced the plate and headed out. I'd never been inside the shop, though I'd seen the guys pulling their farm equipment in and out of it. This seemed like a good time to go explore. When I stepped inside, it was a bit gloomy, despite the overhead fluorescents. It took a minute for my eyes to adjust. The huge tractor was up front, the one that Waylon had driven out to pull me from the cow trough on the night of the infamous topless massage.

Hurrying between that and the side-by-side, I spotted movement at the back of the shop. I hurried back and found Waylon halfway under the hood of an orange muscle car. He had his usual tan Carhartt coveralls on, but the top was peeled down to hang around his waist like jeans. His green thermal shirt showed off his lean muscles. For a minute, I stood there watching him turn a wrench, wondering if it was possible he could be any hotter.

"I brought you a sandwich," I said at last.

Waylon straightened up so fast his head hit the bottom of the hood, and his cowboy hat toppled off, landing in the engine. He growled a curse and plucked it up, replacing it on his head as he turned to me.

"What'd you need?" he asked.

"I..." I trailed off, stung by his short response. I should have been used to it by now. Waylon wasn't a man of many words, and when he did use words, they weren't especially pleasant ones. I tried to imagine what he'd been like with Maria, the ex who had run off and left him for his brother.

"Is that for me?" he asked, plucking the sandwich from the plate. He took a big bite of it and then stood chewing and looking down at it. "What's that taste?"

"It's avocado mayo," I said. "Made with truffle oil."

"Huh." He took another bite.

"Do you like it?" I asked hopefully.

"What's wrong with regular mayo?" he asked, depositing the half-eaten sandwich before turning back to his car.

But I could not be dissuaded that easily. I'd wear him down eventually. No matter how surly he was, I could always get a smile out of him. I sidled up to the car and leaned against it. "So you fix cars?"

"I'm rebuilding the engine," he said, not looking up from his tools.

I tried to pose sexily against the car, but I immediately started sliding back along it. Seriously, looking sexy was difficult while balancing a plate on one hand. I mean, the car was really polished!

"Don't scuff the wax," Waylon said from under the hood.

I propped myself against the side mirror and nibbled at his sandwich. "Did Holden tell you what happened the other night?" I asked.

"What happened?" he asked, not sounding interested at all.

"We kissed."

"Is that right," he said flatly.

"He said you were all okay with...us being together. All four of us. So I guess I'm just wondering...how does it work?"

Finally, Waylon picked up a rag and wiped his hands roughly on it. "It doesn't," he said shortly. "My father's lending us money to save the ranch if we keep you out of trouble for the next two months. That's all."

My heart dropped straight out of my chest and onto the dirty, oily concrete floor. "He's paying you?"

Waylon paused, guilt flickering across his face. "Lending us money," he said after a few seconds. "Not giving it to us."

"So you're babysitting me?" I asked, my humiliation building. My heart was flopping around down there like a fish out of water, just begging him to pick it up or at least put it out of its misery.

"Call it what you want," Waylon said. "You knew we were doing our parents a favor by taking you in."

"I didn't know you were getting *paid*," I said. "I thought we were supposed to get to know our new family a little. That I'd come out here and help out, and you'd let me stay."

"That's what's happening, isn't it?"

"I didn't realize I was such a pain in the ass that you had to get paid to get to know me." To my horror, I felt my lip trembling. My heart was coated with dirt and grime like he was kicking it along the dusty tractor trails through the ranch.

"You're not a pain in the ass, Princess," Waylon said, stepping around the open hood of the car. But I could tell he was just saying it to make me feel better. He didn't sound or look like he meant it one tiny bit.

I gulped, desperately fighting back tears, and stared at anything but his eyes. He had a grease smear on his bare, tan arm. I wanted to freaking lick it. How had I fallen so hard for someone who had to get a paycheck to spend time with me?

But hell, if they were my gigolos, shouldn't I be getting more action?

Waylon took the sandwich from me and took a bite before handing it back. "I didn't ask for money," he said. "I didn't ask for you to come stay here. Our father offered us a deal. Keep you out of trouble, and he'd lend us some money to help keep the ranch going. That's all."

"I just wish I'd known to begin with," I said. "I thought you were all so keen on honesty and openness and not keeping secrets."

"From each other," he said.

Those words stung even deeper than what he'd already said. I wasn't one of them. They were a family who looked out for each other, trusted each other, cared about each other. And I was their stepmother's out-of-control daughter.

"Well, thanks for telling me," I said.

"Amber," he said, his voice gruff. "What happened with Holden shouldn't have happened. He's my brother, but I'll be the first to admit, he's got a weakness when it comes to good-looking women."

"So you think I'm good looking," I teased, desperately trying to sound like I wasn't about to burst into tears.

"What do you want me to say?" he asked. "If you weren't my stepsister, I'd bend you over the hood of this car and fuck you until you screamed loud enough for every neighbor in the next ten miles to come see who was making such a fuss?"

"Oh," I whispered, my thighs quaking at that image.

"That doesn't change the fact that you are my stepsister." He finished the sandwich and picked up the grease rag to wipe his hands again. "Keeping an eye on you means keeping you out of trouble in town, or with the law, but it also means protecting you. Out here, the rules are a little different than what you're used to in New York."

"So you've said. But they don't seem so

different to me."

"People see something they want, they take it," he said. "Ranchers came out here to claim land. There's a little of that spirit left."

"Good to know," I said. "I guess you haven't seen anything you wanted in three years?"

His mouth twisted into a smirk. "Sometimes we want something for a night," he said. "But nothing we've wanted to keep."

I took that as a challenge.

FIVE

Amber

After talking to Waylon, I decided not to tell my
stepbrothers about their creepy ranch hand. They
would do anything to save their ranch, and I didn't
want to be a reason they failed. After all, if they fired
Grimes, the whole ranch would fall apart. They'd told
me that themselves. And besides all that, he'd been
here for forty years, and I'd been here less than a
month. He belonged there. If I told on him, he'd
probably do something worse than calling me a
whore.

So I went back to the house and had a glass of
wine. Okay, maybe it was two. And they were pretty
full.

When a car drove up, I got up from the table
and peeked out. A gold Cadillac sedan sat in the
gravel area in front of the house.

Great. Another neighbor.

A woman with frosted blonde hair and a

puffy parka climbed out of the car and tottered across the gravel in heels. She looked to be in her forties or fifties, and from her car and her bag, comfortably living but not extravagantly wealthy. I opened the door before she could knock.

"Well, hello, dear," she said, clattering up the steps in her heels. "I thought I'd come pay a visit. See what all the gossip was about in town."

"Oh, hi, then," I said as she bustled past me and into the house.

"I figured the boys would be out this time of day, so we could have a little girl talk," she said, hanging her coat on the rack behind the door.

Okay, then. A bit presumptuous, but whatever.

"I don't know if I'm the best one to share gossip," I said. "I've only been to town once, and all we did was buy a new phone and some hardware."

"Oh, honey, I'm not here to gossip with you about other people," she said. "I'm here to see with my own eyes what other people are gossiping about."

I gulped. "Other people are gossiping about me?"

"Well, of course," she said. "You're new to the area. Not to mention, a pretty girl like you living with three handsome single men."

"Uh huh." I wasn't drunk, but I wasn't sober enough for this conversation. What if I said something wrong, like, *hell yeah, they're hotter than hell and I want to make up for lost time and do all three of them?*

27

"Aren't you going to offer me a drink?" she asked, standing by the coat rack.

"Sure, I guess," I said, wondering if the boys would like this gossipy stranger snooping around in their house. I'd have to watch the old coot if she went to the bathroom.

"Manners are a little lacking," she commented as I led her into the kitchen.

"Wine?" I asked, motioning to the bottle and my empty glass, which were still on the table.

"Heavens no," she said, sounding truly scandalized. "It's barely past lunch time."

"Never stopped me," I said with a grin, hoping she'd lighten up and join me.

"I see that," the woman said, glaring disapprovingly at my glass.

"We've also got beer," I offered.

Instead of laughing, she frowned harder. Craptastic. That hadn't worked at all. If we both got a little tipsy, we'd be on a more even playing field. Maybe we'd even be friends. I could use someone to stop by, have a cocktail, and chat every once in a while, even if she was the neighborhood gossip. That would serve Waylon right for being a dick to me.

"Or tea," I said weakly. "Soda?"

"I'll take a Diet Coke, please and thank you," she said, pulling out a chair and sitting down at the table. "And throw another log on the fire if you don't mind."

"Okay, then." I handed over the can of Diet

Coke, which she scowled at. "Diet Coke, right?" I asked when she didn't reach for it.

"I'll take a glass and some ice, if you don't mind," she said.

"Guess I'm not the only one who needs to learn manners," I muttered as I grabbed a glass and filled it with ice. When the drink was up to her standards, I turned to the wood stove.

"They told me you were easy on the eyes," she said. "That might be a good thing for my boys if my ex-husband hadn't gone and married that senator. It does no good for stepsiblings to be the same age."

I had opened the door to the fire, and I almost pitched headlong into the coals.

"What did you just say?" I squeaked.

"I said it's no good for you to be the same age as my boys. I'm sure they could use some good women around here, but it's not doing anyone any favors to put a pretty girl in front of three lonely men and tell them they can't have her. I don't know what that man was thinking."

"You're their mother?" I reached out to steady myself and almost put my hand on top of the stove. Considering my history with mishaps since I'd arrived, I figured I should get away from any hot surfaces, so I stumbled to the table and collapsed into a chair. I'd been rude to their mother! I wanted to die.

"Of course I'm their mother," she said. "Who did you think I was? You smell like you're three sheets to the wind, but try to keep up, dear."

Oh my God, oh my God, it's their mother. What do I do?

"Yes, ma'am," I said. It was useless trying to think of the right thing to do. I'd had exactly one long-term boyfriend who introduced me to his mother, and she'd hated me. Heaven forbid a girl like to get her drink on and hit up the dance floor every now and then. You'd think I was a seasoned criminal, the way Charlie's mother had treated me.

And now here I was, making a total fool of myself in front of the mother of all three of the men I was currently crushing on. I'd never even had a chance.

Before I could dig my hole any deeper, I pulled out my phone and sent a covert text to the guys. After falling in the cow water, I'd made sure to get all their numbers and have them at the ready both individually and as a group text in case of emergency. I did seem especially prone to them on the ranch. And if being stuck in a house with their mother wasn't a dire emergency, I didn't know what was.

*

"Mother," Sawyer said, striding in a few minutes later. "How nice of you to drop in on us like this."

"I didn't know I needed an invitation," she said. "I gave you life, after all?"

"How could I forget," Sawyer said, rolling his eyes over her head.

Holden came in a minute later, stomped his boots, and appeared in the kitchen. He was breathing hard, and his eyes moved from one of us to the next. "Is everyone okay?" he asked. "I got your SOS text."

I winced, cursing him silently. Now his mother was going to hate me even more.

"Is that so?" their mother asked, eyeing me.

"I can see why," Holden said, crossing the room to sweep his mother up into a bear hug. "It would have been just awful to miss you, Mama."

"A real tragedy," Sawyer said.

"Thanks for letting us know, sis," Holden said, shooting me a meaningful look over his mother's head. As if I'd tell her what I'd told Waylon.

The next minute, Waylon came rushing in and pulled up so short his boot heels nearly left skid marks on the kitchen floor. "Lidia," he said, giving her a curt nod.

"None of that," she said. "You best call me Mama. I'm the only one the good Lord gave you, and I don't plan on going anywhere anytime soon."

"Fine," he grunted.

"Unless you're planning to replace me with that senator your father's gone and married."

Before I could think, a snort escaped me. They all looked my way. "Trust me, you don't need to worry about that," I said.

"Speaking ill of her own mother," Lidia said, shaking her head.

"Would you like something to eat while you're here?" Holden asked.

"You should try some of Amber's special

avocado-truffle oil mayonnaise," Waylon said.

I shot him a death glare, but his poker face never wavered. Damn, he was good.

"Kids these days," Lidia said. "What's wrong with regular old mayonnaise?"

"Just wait until you try it," Waylon said, heading for the fridge. "It's to die for."

I slid over to the counter and planted my hands on my hips, waiting for Waylon to turn from the fridge. When he did, I hissed, "What are you doing?"

"Making a sandwich for my mother," he said, a picture of innocence.

"She's going to hate it," I whispered.

"If you're lucky," he muttered. "If she likes it, she'll be back every day. And I can't lock her out like Mrs. Grimes."

"So tell me, how are you all getting along?" Lidia asked behind us.

"Famously," Sawyer said.

Only Holden had sat down at the table beside his mom. It was sort of sweet how genuinely pleased to see her he seemed, though I couldn't say I shared that sentiment.

"No squabbles? After the last time you had a woman here, I can't say I approve."

"Amber's nearly our sister, though," Sawyer said, catching my eye and shooting me a wink.

Lidia nodded. "That's good to hear. Can't have a repeat of that last one."

"Trust me, Mother, that will never happen again," Waylon said, his jaw set. He was the only one who hadn't talked to me about Maria, who had broken all their hearts.

"Thank the Lord," Lidia said. "But I still don't know if I think this is a good idea. The way people talk around here…"

"Amber's helping out with the horses," Holden said. "She's good at it, too. In fact, she's pretty damn near the perfect sister."

"Like the little sister we never had," Sawyer agreed, his eyes sparkling with merriment.

"Hmph," Lidia said. "Could have fooled me."

"You may have caught me at a bad moment," I said.

"I'll say."

Oh no. I could feel a verbal torrent building inside me. I was helpless to stop it.

"But that doesn't mean I'm a bad person," I went on. "I actually have been helping with the horses, though I can't say I'm keen on making that old buzzard's life any easier. By that I mean Grimes, not you. Not that you're old. Or a buzzard. I just mean, Grimes is a total creep. But I'm sure you know that, seeing that you lived here at some point, I'm assuming. Right? Or did it skip a generation, like twins, and go straight from your dad to your kids?"

Lidia opened her mouth, then closed it again. Finally she said, "Well. I guess you could keep her around for entertainment value if nothing else."

Now I didn't just have to prove myself worthy to all the guys, but to their mother? Craptastic.

"She's only here for a couple more months," Waylon said, delivering a sandwich to his mother and one to me.

"And then you can get your payday and live happily ever after," I said, remembering I was mad at him.

"Sit, eat. It'll take the edge off," he muttered when I gave him a withering look.

"Well, the talk in town's just getting started," Lidia said. "And I don't think it's proper, her being what she is."

"What I am?" I asked indignantly.

Waylon's hand closed on my shoulder, firm and commanding. "If people want to gossip, they're going to gossip," he said, facing his mother.

Sawyer tipped his chair back, his legs sprawling under the table. "If it's not this, it's something else," he said. "You can't stop gossip any more than you can stop the wind from blowing."

"It's true," I said. "You know why the gossip column is always full? It's not because there's always something scandalous going on. It's because it has to be. There's a space for it, an audience for it, and it's the job of the writers to fill the column with something. They have to find something to talk about."

Lidia narrowed her eyes at me, but she didn't say anything.

"Whatever people in town say about us, they've been saying for years," Sawyer said. "Doesn't bother us."

"Does it bother you, Amber?" Holden asked.

I shrugged. "My parents are both in politics. People have been talking about me since I was born."

"Well, aren't we humble," Lidia said.

"Were you married to Senator Westling when he was a senator?" I asked. "If you have tips on being invisible in politics, I'd love to hear them."

"All I'm saying is that people will talk," Lidia said. "I think my sons deserve to know that. You know they caused quite a local scandal a few years ago."

"So I've heard."

"I'm going back to work," Waylon said. "I don't have time for gossip." When his hand left my shoulder, I felt woozy again, and desperate for his hand to steady me. But he stomped out of the kitchen, leaving me with his two brothers and his mother.

"I just think you might be happier someplace else," Lidia said to me. "My ex-husband has no right to force you to live with these boys. And neither does your mother."

"She didn't force me to," I said. "It's a break for me, that's all. I needed to get away, anyway. And in case you hadn't noticed, I've been decorating around here. I've never seen such a bare bones place as this. The only decoration in the whole house is a rack of antlers and a bear skin on the floor. It looks like a hunting lodge, not a home."

"Well," Lidia said with a huff. "That's not my style, but they are boys."

"Doesn't mean the place couldn't use a woman's touch."

Sawyer smiled at me. "Trust me, Mother, Amber's no trouble for us."

"Depends on your definition of trouble," she muttered.

Ain't that the truth, I thought, trying not to openly ogle Sawyer as he peeled off his jacket.

SIX

Amber

When Holden took their mother outside to show her some new farm equipment, I finally breathed again. "Sorry about that," Sawyer said, taking a seat beside me. "Our mother can be a handful."

"All women are," I said lightly. But inside, I was fuming.

"Here, I think you've earned another glass," Sawyer said, pouring some wine and handing it to me.

I took the wine and set it down carefully, so I wouldn't spill any when I turned and punched him in the shoulder. "You could have warned me," I hissed. "I made a total ass of myself."

"You do have a pretty nice ass…"

"Not funny," I growled. "She hates me!"

"Aww, no one could hate you, Princess," he said, reaching out and slowly tucking a strand of hair behind my ear. His touch lingered on my cheek.

"This doesn't feel like brotherly love," I whispered.

"The house isn't the only thing that could use a woman's touch," he said, leaning closer.

"Is that so?" I turned in my chair to face him.

Sawyer pressed his forehead to mine, his eyes cast down at my wine-stained lips.

Suddenly breathless, I lifted my hands and steadied myself by clutching his massive arms. My god, I'd never found muscles so sexy in my life. Slowly, he moved the tip of his nose back and forth across mine, a smile beginning on his lips. Tingles spread down my spine, and my back arched, wanting to get closer. I clenched my knees together against the heat swelling between them.

His hand slid from my ear to the back of my neck, and he closed his eyes and inhaled deeply.

"Kiss me," I whispered.

He did. His kiss wasn't tentative and soft like Holden's. It was passionate and forceful. His tongue took command of mine, and I was lost. My pussy throbbed as he angled his head sideways to taste my mouth more deeply. I'd never been kissed like that in my life—as if he wanted to know every millimeter of my mouth, my tongue, my lips. As if he wanted to claim them for his own. A sound escaped my mouth, somewhere between a moan and a whimper.

Embarrassing. But who the hell cared? I was too busy kissing my stepbrother to worry about it. I mean, sure I'd made out with Charlie tons. Usually I was desperately trying to get him to show just a little bit of passion, instead of doing everything in the mechanical way he had. He kissed like he'd researched how to kiss on the internet, and he was following the steps exactly, and no deviation was allowed.

Sawyer's kiss was nothing but passion, his tongue claiming mine, his breath coming fast. He bent me backwards with the force of it, and I dropped my hand to his knee to steady myself. His skin was hot through his jeans, and I wanted to run my hand all the way up his thigh and touch him the way I'd done the night we'd slept on the living room floor together.

Before I could, he pulled away.

I wanted to howl in frustration. I grabbed the front of his shirt, trying to keep the kiss going, but he pried my fingers loose. "We'd better stop now, or I won't be able to," he said, breathing hard.

"Who said I'd stop you?"

He cocked an eyebrow and grinned. "I don't think my mother would be happy if she came back and found me eating *you* on the kitchen table."

A shiver of desire went through me at the thought of him kissing my pussy the way he'd just kissed my mouth.

"You better not have been thinking about her when you kissed me," I said.

Sawyer made a face. "Never," he said. "But I might have enjoyed it a little more knowing how pissed she'd be if she knew."

"You're terrible," I said.

"You're irresistible," he countered. "Too irresistible to be my stepsister."

I smiled up at him and batted my lashes. "Does that mean you don't want me here?"

"Wanting you is not the problem," he said, pushing back from the table. He held out a hand, and when I took it, he pulled me effortlessly to my feet. I stumbled against him, and he laughed and caught me around the waist, pulling my body against his. "Or maybe it is," he growled, nuzzling my ear before releasing me.

"Maybe that last glass of wine wasn't such a good idea after all," I said, suddenly breathless again. I gripped his arms—God, his arms were great—and he steadied me on my feet.

"Want to go lie down?" he said. "I could probably make an excuse to my mother."

"Only if you'll come lie down with me," I said.

What can I say, the wine made me bold.

Sawyer laughed. "If you weren't intoxicated, and my mother wouldn't notice, I'd take you up on that. But I think she'd notice if we both disappeared."

"She'd be scandalized," I said. "Isn't that what you want?"

"We better join them before they start thinking we're in here kissing at the kitchen table," he said with a wink. He took my hand and led me to the door, his grip firm and strong around mine. I didn't want to let go, but I figured holding hands was not acceptable brother-sister behavior beyond age six or something.

We emerged from the house just in time to see Holden and Lidia walking out of the barn. A flare of guilt shot through me. Seconds earlier, I'd been kissing my stepbrother with no shame. Actually, I'd been propositioning him.

"I seriously need my vibrator," I muttered.

"What?" Sawyer squawked.

Laughter burst out of me before I could stop it. "What? Nothing. I didn't say anything."

"I think you did," he said, his eyes sparkling with amusement.

"I definitely didn't say whatever you think I said."

"How do you know what I think you said?"

"Because I can see it on your face," I said. "Now shut up and let's go charm the pants off your mom. Not literally, though, this is already weird enough without adding any Oedipus shit to the mix."

"We're in agreement on that one," he muttered as we joined the other two.

"Your brother was just showing me the horses," Lidia said. Her eyes met mine, narrowing as she studied me.

Craptastic. I must be blushing, or flushed from the kiss. Or was there some kind of mark he'd made by kissing me so hard, like a hickey on my lips? I wanted to touch them to make sure they weren't swollen, but that would be a dead giveaway. But she could definitely smell my guilt like a bloodhound on the trail.

This was bad. Why hadn't I gone and laid down when Sawyer told me to?

I peeked at him from the corner of my eye as we headed for the guys' shop. Were his lips stained from the wine I'd drunk?

When we stepped inside, Waylon was under the hood of his old car again. We made our way to the back of the shop where he was working.

"Oh, this is beautiful," Lidia said, walking around the car and admiring it.

Waylon grunted.

I did a double-take. It was a pumpkin-colored boxy old thing with a bar running right through the middle of the top, so it wasn't even a real convertible. Not that I knew anything about cars. People in New York didn't really drive. My parents both had cars, but they never took them out of the garage unless they were going out to the Hamptons or upstate for a weekend. When she did use her car, Mom hired a driver so she could ride in the backseat and nurse her gin-and-valium hangover while pretending to work on emails.

Lidia leaned over and peered through the glass top.

"Leather," Waylon said, glowering at his mother.

"A '78," she said, tapping on the glass with

one manicured nail. My mother got shellac manicures, short and practical, in a neutral color that would last out a season, like lilac or nude. Lidia's nails looked like she'd smashed a piece of candy corn onto the end of each finger.

"Hurst Hatch?" she asked.

Whatever a Hurst Hatch was, it seemed to wake Waylon from his stew of resentment. He straightened up and actually smiled, though I could tell he was fighting it. "Fisher units," he said.

"This is in excellent condition," she said. "Are you keeping the color?"

"This isn't the original color," he said. "Come here." He opened up the door and she went over and bent down, and they started talking about cars like they were fancy cocktails they couldn't wait to try.

I turned to Sawyer. "I don't get it."

"It's their thing," he said with a shrug. While his mother and brother were busy looking at something inside the door, Sawyer took my hand and gave it a squeeze. When I glanced at him in surprise, he licked his lips and then grinned, squeezing my hand for another second before letting go. A shiver of naughty feeling crept through me. For the rest of the twenty minutes we stood there, my body was aware of his every movement even when I wasn't sneaking glances at him.

Finally, Waylon and his mother remembered we were there, and we all headed towards the door. I followed Sawyer, my gaze riveted on his ass. How had

I never noticed a guy's ass before? The muscles in Sawyer's ass hypnotized me as they flexed with each step. So much so that I kinda-sorta ran into one of the huge tractor tires.

I bounced off the tire and went reeling straight towards the wall, which was covered in shovels and rakes and hoes. Flailing my arms, I tried to right myself, but I only managed to grab the handle of a pitchfork, which came loose from its hanger. Off balance, I plowed forward, careening straight for Lidia like a savage warrior about to impale the enemy.

SEVEN

Waylon

By the time we got the tools hung up and Amber dusted off, my mother had calmed down.

"We're not laughing at you," Holden assured her before turning to Amber. "Or you."

Amber stood there looking so damn cute with her stunned, bewildered expression. She hadn't reached our Ma, but had fallen flat on her face in front of the lot of us.

"It's safe to say you're not curbing her drinking ways," our mother said in a huff.

"She's fine," I said. "She'll sleep it off and have a headache when she wakes up. No one ever died of a hangover."

I thought it strange that a self-professed party girl could get sloppy from a few glasses of wine, but seeing Amber swaying on her feet was proof enough.

"I wasn't trying to stab you," she said for the hundredth time. "I swear!"

Lidia narrowed her eyes at our stepsister. "I don't know about you living out here," she said. "It may not be New York, but looks like you've found new ways to go wild. I don't know what my ex was thinking, sending you out here. But I think it would be best if you came back to town with me."

"Why?" Amber's blue eyes widened. Damn, she looked innocent. Too damn innocent to be living with the likes of us.

"To live with me," Lidia said. "It's far more proper than you living out here, doing as you please. My sons have plenty of work on the ranch without having to keep an eye on your questionable behavior all day."

"But...but we're not even related," Amber protested. "I mean, not that I'm related to your sons, but at least legally, I'm their sister. I don't even know you."

"I think what she's saying, Ma, is that she'd like a chance to get to know us a little better," Sawyer said, draping an arm around Amber's shoulder. I could see it was to steady her on her feet more than anything, and I gave him a slight nod to thank him.

"I'm not asking what she'd like," Lidia said. "She's in no state to make decisions, and even if she was, her judgment obviously leaves something to be desired."

"You're making a big deal out of nothing," Sawyer said.

"Her judgment is fine," I added, though I

tended to agree with Lidia on that one. It was something else altogether that we desired, something that relied on her lack of good judgment. For the hundredth time, I cursed the shit luck that had made her our stepsister. We'd been looking for a woman with her kind of questionable judgment for years. A woman who wouldn't pass judgment on us, who might think this insane lifestyle we were after was something desirable. If only we could find someone openminded enough to give it a shot, someone who didn't give a fuck what people in town thought.

In short, the opposite of Amber fucking Durant.

"It would be good for her to be under a more watchful eye," Lidia said. "She'll learn a thing or two from living with a parent who sets her straight when she makes mistakes instead of letting it get to the point where she has to be hidden away across the country."

"We don't mind looking out for her," Holden said quietly. "We like having her around."

"I'm sure you do," Lidia said, giving Amber a critical look. "Honey, you aren't pregnant, are you? Because I know a thing or two about babies."

"I'm not pregnant," Amber snapped. "For your information, I've never even had sex. So I guess I'm not the spawn of Satan after all, just a regular old lush."

She was a virgin? Fucking hell. How much worse could this get?

Sawyer choked on the v-bomb, covering it with a forced cough. Holden's face blanched.

"All the more reason not to let the gossip tarnish your reputation," Ma said. "Come on, honey. I'll take good care of you and keep you out of trouble."

"What's she going to do at your place?" Sawyer asked. "Go to bridge club and bingo night? She's eighteen, Ma, not eighty."

I looked at that girl, standing there so innocently, swaying after only a couple glasses of wine. And I knew if she went to live with our mother, we'd never get to know her. We'd never know if she was all talk or if she'd meant what she said to Holden about being interested in all of us.

That was a good thing. We couldn't have her, even if we wanted her, so there was no point in finding out, only to have her ripped away in two months' time.

I knew exactly how my mother's controlling style had stifled and smothered us all our lives. Hell, we were grown men and she was still here meddling, trying to make decisions for us and Amber both. If we let her take Amber, Amber would never forgive us. More than that, Dad wouldn't. We'd promised to take care of her, and now, as I thought of the tedium of her days with our mother, I knew that would break her wild spirit.

But what we wanted to do to her would wreck her, body and soul.

EIGHT

Amber

I looked from one of my stepbrothers to the next. Sawyer was going to fight for me to stay, as evidenced by our united stand. He had wrapped a protective arm around me, and I could have kissed him for it. Well, if I hadn't already kissed him. Oops.

Holden was watching me and his mother with a troubled expression, as if it hurt him to go against his mother's wishes and vote for me to stay. But he'd been the one to hint at a relationship, hint at something more than a lusty kiss. And he'd defended me to his mother, whom he clearly loved. My heart warmed at the thought.

Only Waylon hadn't spoken up in my defense. When I turned to him, his hard, dark eyes glowered back at me. I gulped, quaking in my Ugg boots. There was no way he was going to agree, and they'd already told me, nothing happened around here without a unanimous decision. Which meant I was fucked, but not in the good way.

Although something in his eyes hinted at a dark desire. Under that steely exterior he must have formed when his fiancé ran off with his brother, I was sure that there was a storm of passion that I could unleash. The thought made me shiver in more ways than one.

I tore my eyes away from Waylon, focusing instead of Lidia. She was looking at me like she couldn't wait to get me away from her precious sons. But surely they wouldn't send me off to live with this horrid woman. I'd die. I had enough conflict with my own mother, and she let me do pretty much anything I wanted, as long as I didn't end up in a gossip column. Or, you know, the police station.

This woman was looking at me like she was already making plans to lock me up in a nunnery because I was still young and God forbid, had a sexual thought in my head about her undeniably sexy sons. And frankly, I'd had quite enough of being locked away from who I was. Yes, I wanted to have sex. I wanted to have so much sex that if she could've read my mind, she'd have dropped dead from shock.

That didn't mean I couldn't control myself. If I had to hole up in my room and order vibrators online for the next two months, that's what I'd do. But I was not going with her.

"Well," Lidia said to Holden after a long silence. "I'm glad you boys have your opinions, but your oldest brother has the most say in this ranch, and he knows you don't have time for all this nonsense on top of running the place. The last thing you need is the headache of raising a teenage girl with wild ways. Isn't that right, Waylon?"

His jaw tensed, and his eyes settled on mine, piercing through me. Suddenly I felt like I was standing in front of him stripped naked again, frozen and at his mercy. But this time, it felt completely different.

"I want to stay," I said before he could answer. "I'll help with the horses, and decorate the house when you're out, and when you're in the house, I'll stay in my room and be so quiet you won't even know I'm there."

"We'll know you're there," Sawyer murmured.

"You don't have to," I said, pulling away from him and focusing on staying steady and sounding reasonable, sober, and responsible, just like everyone wanted me to be. "I came out here to get away, and I admit, drinking today was obviously a mistake. But I don't want to make anyone's life harder. No one is responsible for me except me. And I'm going to do better from now on. If I mess up again, I'll come live with you, Lidia. Does that sound fair?"

She opened her mouth, but before she could speak, Waylon did. "That's fair."

I gaped at him. He was the last one I expected to speak up for me. I figured I'd have to fight it out with Sawyer, and maybe Holden, though he'd probably cave to his brother and mother after a couple minutes. Instead, Waylon had shut his mother down with two words.

She huffed and puffed for a minute, but when Waylon stepped up beside me and put a hand on my shoulder, she shut her mouth and glared. Sawyer reclaimed his spot at my other side, this time setting a hand on my shoulder like Waylon had. Holden stepped up on Waylon's other side, and we all faced Lidia together, an impenetrable wall of stepsiblingly love. If that was a thing.

"She stays," Waylon said.

Lidia nodded, her mouth tight. "You're going to regret this. Mark my words."

"They won't," I assured her. "I'm not going to do a single thing that could get me into trouble. Before you know it, I'll be gone, and you'll all go on like I was never here at all."

"The first I hear about you in town, I'm coming right back up here," she said. "You can either come live with me, or go on home to New York and your own mother can figure out what to do with you besides saddling someone else with your behavior. You'll be her problem then. And don't you go thinking I've forgotten you're up here. I'll be keeping an eye out, be keeping my ears open for any gossip. You can't hide anything in a place this small. If anything happens, I'll hear about it."

For some reason, I was sure she wasn't just talking about getting tipsy. It was weird, because in New York, there were people all around me all the time. On the sidewalk, in stores and clubs and restaurants, even in our building, where people lived above and below us. Here, it seemed there was nothing but space, endless stretches of open land that went on for miles, and yet, I felt more watched, more claustrophobic.

In New York, no one really cared about anyone else's business unless you literally murdered someone. Or, apparently, if you threw eggs at a spoiled rich boy and his car. But that was beside the point.

In Wyoming, it seemed everyone wanted to know exactly what I was doing at all times, and they all wanted to pass judgment. They'd go out of their way to find me and check on what I was doing, which was totally weird to me. I was used to people who were so busy that if I passed out on the sidewalk, they'd just walk around me...if that.

"I'm sure you'll be the first to hear every tidbit of gossip that happens in this county," Sawyer said. "And we appreciate your concern, Ma, but we're grown men and we can take care of ourselves, and between the three of us, probably one teenage girl, too."

"But you're welcome to drop in for a visit anytime," Holden hurried to add. "We love having you, Mama."

With one last suspicious once-over, she turned to walk back to her car. Holden jogged to join her.

"I think I better go lie down, after all," I said.

"That might not be a bad idea," Sawyer said. "Can't have you going after anyone else with a pitchfork."

"You jerk," I said, punching his arm. "You're the one who gave me that third glass of wine. And you know the pitchfork was an accident."

"I think we were all hoping you'd at least skewer her foot," he said with a wink.

"Yeah, because then she'd be bedridden, and I'd have to wait on her as penance."

"Let me walk you in," Waylon said, nodding at the house. "Make sure you get there in one piece."

I shot Sawyer a pleading look over my shoulder, but he didn't seem concerned that his mean brother was leading me away. I guessed that was shitty—Waylon had saved me on more than one occasion. But while the others had warmed up to me, he'd been more surly as the days went on.

"Thanks for taking my side," I said. "Even if it was just to nettle your mom."

He grunted in response.

"I know you just want me here so your dad will send you a check," I said. "But I meant what I said. You won't even know I'm here."

"We'll know you're here," he growled, shooting me a dark look.

"Sorry, I'm not a magician, I can't just make myself disappear. If I was, I'd send myself back in time and undo that stupid arrest."

I felt cheap, somehow, and humiliated that I'd thought it was something more than it was. A job. To save their precious ranch. I should have known. He was all business. The ranch came first. No wonder he hadn't liked my idea about renting out the four cabins that sat empty behind the house He knew they had money coming their way if they kept me under lock and key.

But I was sick of being locked up. Charlie had practically put me in a museum. I wasn't going to let anyone else do that to me. I would have my run of the ranch, even if I had to avoid my stepbrothers during the few hours in the evening when they were downstairs. We always ate dinner together, but otherwise, I often didn't see them for most of the day.

When we reached my room, I stumbled in and threw myself face down on the bed. I expected the door to close behind me, but it didn't. After a minute, I felt my boots being tugged off.

"I know you'd rather Sawyer have walked you up," Waylon said flatly. "I thought it would be best for our mother not to see one of us take a special interest in you."

"You think Sawyer takes a special interest in me?" I blurted out. Then I winced, thinking I probably should have said I didn't like Sawyer more. I didn't. It was just that Waylon could be a little...unpredictable. And scary.

"We all take an interest in you," he said, setting my boots under the edge of the bed. "And I'm not trying to make you disappear. But it's impossible not to know you're in here, in this bedroom, every night. Your presence permeates the house. It's impossible not to feel a woman in our house when we all go to bed alone."

And with that, he strode out of the room and closed the door.

Craptastic. Just when I thought I could be good and stay away from them, he had to tempt me with that image. I imagined them all in their beds, lonely, wanting to tiptoe down the hall and slip into my bed as badly as I wanted to visit each of theirs.

Fuck. I had it bad, and it showed no signs of going away.

NINE

Amber

Lying down made the world spin a bit too much, so I sat up. Waylon had gone, and the house was quiet. The boys would be out on the ranch now, checking on the cows, closing off one pasture and opening another, moving the herd...whatever they'd been doing when their mother arrived. I figured it hadn't been moving the herd, since Waylon had been working on his car. It must be a slow day.

I went downstairs and finished the sandwich Waylon had made for me. I noticed his mother hadn't eaten much of hers, either. Apparently, avocado-truffle oil mayo was too trendy for Wyomingites. When I'd finished my sandwich, I felt a little more stable. But then the humiliation set in. I couldn't believe I'd gotten drunk again and screwed up my life even more. Well, I could, as that was pretty much the norm. Except for almost stabbing someone with a pitchfork. That was brand spanking new Amber behavior.

I plunked onto the couch and pulled the knit throw off the back, pulling it tight around me. The blanket was a new addition I thought livened up the place, and now it was coming in handy. I snuggled down into it, and finally fell asleep.

When I woke, it was to the smell of frying meat and the sound of music in the kitchen. With the blanket still clutched around me, I got up and trudged in.

"Hey, Princess," Sawyer said, shooting me a smile. He was at the stove, where two pans steamed and sizzled. "Up for some cowboy tacos?"

"Ungh," I managed.

Sawyer laughed and stepped over, kissing me on the forehead before turning to grab a bag of tortillas from the fridge. "I'll take that as a hell yes."

"Need some help?" I asked, trying to wet the inside of my mouth with my parched tongue.

"Nah, sit down, put your feet up, and enjoy watching the master."

"Your humbleness always astounds me," I muttered, flopping into a chair.

"Want a beer?"

"I think I'm good on the alcohol for today."

Sawyer laughed as he threw a dash of pepper into each pan. "Three glasses of wine isn't that bad."

"Yeah, my glasses were more like doubles. So by the time I had yours, that was like my fifth glass. And it was, like…noon."

"Wait until we get a real snow," he said. "If we're stuck in here, it's whiskey time all the time."

I imagined what would happen if we all got drunk together. It wasn't exactly an unpleasant thought. But I'd promised to be good, and I was going to.

"Can I go ring the dinner bell?" I asked, standing.

"Sure thing, Princess," he said. "Dinner's about on."

After eating and cleaning up the kitchen, we sat around the fire in the living room, though I declined the invitation to have a beer with them. My head was aching from all the red wine I'd consumed earlier.

"Should I go upstairs?" I asked. "I really will hang out in my room when you're here if it bothers you to have me around. And you really don't have to babysit me. I'm sorry about drinking your wine, too. It won't happen again."

"We don't want you to hang out in your room," Sawyer said, taking a swig of beer. "You're a guest here, and you're welcome to all the wine you can drink."

"Just maybe not when our mother is around," Holden said, offering me a small smile.

"Okay, in my defense, she wasn't here when I started drinking," I said. "And I blame you, Sawyer. If you hadn't given me an extra glass…"

"You wouldn't have gone after her with a

pitchfork?" he asked.

They all laughed, but it was warm laughter, and I found myself joining them. A safe feeling of comradery filled the room. Was I part of this now? For the moment, I was one of them, accepted and embraced. I looked around at the three of them, my stepbrothers. Seeing them all laughing together, happy and relaxed, filled my chest with an unbearable sweetness.

We stayed up talking until it grew late, and I nodded off. I woke to find Waylon bending over me, sliding an arm under my legs and one under my back.

"What are you doing?" I asked sleepily, draping my arm over his shoulder.

"I'm laying you down, that's all," he said. "Unless you want me to carry you up to your room."

"You'd do that?" I asked, snuggling into his shoulder.

He made a noncommittal sound in response.

"Are you ever going to let me see what's under that tough-guy act?" I asked, pinching his nose.

He jerked his head away and stood, looking down at me with a frown. "I guess now that you're awake, you can make it to your room on your own."

"I think I'll sleep here," I said, pulling the blanket from the back of the couch.

For a minute, he just stood watching me like he thought I was up to something. So I smiled innocently up at him, snuggling deeper under the blanket.

"I'll throw a couple more logs on, then," he said after a long moment.

While he went outside to get more wood, I shuffled over to the fire and sat on the bearskin rug, the blanket wrapped around me like a cocoon. Waylon's boots tromped on the steps outside, and then the door blew open hard, a blast of icy air sweeping across the room. Little flakes of snow skittered across the floor before melting on the hardwood. Waylon reached behind him with one foot, caught the door with his cowboy boot, and kicked it closed.

When he knelt before the fire, I could see a slight flush on his stubbly cheeks from his short trip outside. Two minutes outside and his face looked frozen. He didn't comment on my moving from the couch. He just concentrated on rekindling the coals to get the fire going, leaning down and blowing on them until flames licked up against the cold logs.

At last, when the flames were flickering along the logs, he sat back on his heels. "That'll do you fine."

"Will it?" I asked, reaching out one foot to poke his calf with my toe.

He looked down at my bare foot like it was an alien. After a long moment, he raised his head. "What are you doing?" he asked quietly.

"Nothing," I said lightly.

"I'd better get to bed," he said, staring at my foot again.

"Wait," I said, gulping. If I wanted him to be real with me, I had to be willing to do the same with him. Which was a lot harder than I expected—it was easier when I was half-drunk and fully pissed.

He waited, watching my face with a bland, blank expression.

I swallowed again. "Do you want to stay with me…a little longer?"

He waited again, as if he expected me to answer the question for him. After a minute, I shifted and dropped my gaze from his. "I mean, you don't have to. I know you get up early, and you'll probably have to haul hay for the cows tomorrow, and do all kinds of stuff I don't even know goes into running a ranch. It's fine, don't worry about it. I'm still going to sit down here, though. I'll watch the fire until it dies down a little. Thanks for doing that, by the way. Getting the fire going for me. That was really nice of you. Oh my God, do you milk the cows? I just realized I've never seen you doing that. Do you think you could teach me?"

"All right," he said.

"You'll teach me to milk a cow?" I asked, pulling the blanket down around my waist. I could just imagine the great cow pictures I could send Haley if I milked one.

"I'll stay a minute, if you need someone to talk to." He sat on the bearskin rug, leaving a space between us big enough for another person to fit, and leaned back on his hands.

"Oh," I said, laughing a little as I tried not to stare at his muscles. God, they all had the most gorgeous arms. It must be a family trait. "That's just my rambling," I said weakly.

"I noticed."

"Be nice," I said, opening the blanket. "You don't make it easy, you know."

"What?"

"Talking to you. You're so quiet."

"Doesn't that make it easier?"

"You'd think." When he didn't move, I scooted over and draped the blanket around his shoulders, too.

"Did the others go to bed?"

He nodded.

"How come you're still up?"

"Can't sleep lately."

"Because I'm here?" I blurted out.

To my surprise, he nodded again, not denying it.

A gust of wind howled by the house, rattling it like old bones. The fire crackled in the fireplace, and I leaned my head on his shoulder. He didn't grab me up into a passionate embrace and kiss me like a cowboy who hadn't seen a woman in months. But he didn't tell me to fuck off, either.

"What do you want to do now?" I asked, my heart hammering. He was so close. I could smell him, an outdoorsy smell like freshly chopped wood and hay.

Waylon smirked and slid down under the blanket, pulling me down next to him. He lay on his side, propped up on one elbow. "You really want to know?"

Suddenly, I was shaking all over. "I really want to know."

"You'll know I'm a filthy animal if I tell you."

"I already know you're a filthy animal," I teased, but inside, my heart was slamming.

"Okay." Waylon licked his lips. "I want to see you kneeling on the rug in front of the fire."

I swallowed hard. "Right now?"

"I'm just getting started," he said, his eyes gleaming in the firelight. "Slow down there, Princess."

"Oh," I breathed.

"I want you on all fours," he said. "Naked. And I want you to arch your back, and turn and look at me over your shoulder, in that sexy way you have, with your hair falling all around you, and your ass in the air. I want to see you reach back and touch yourself until your cunt is glistening wet. And then I want to crawl across the floor to you, spread it open, and taste you."

I could feel myself getting wet just listening to him. His eyes were locked on mine, intense and burning with desire. My own face was hot, but I couldn't look away.

"Is that all?" I whispered breathlessly.

"No," he said. "Then I want to fuck you."

His hand moved under the blanket, finding

my breast and cupping it. His fingers grazed over my shirt until he found the edge of my bra. He tugged it down and pinched my nipple through my shirt.

A stab of desire shot straight from my nipple to my clit. "We could," I breathed. "No one has to know."

"Oh, but they will," he said, rolling my nipple slowly between his thumb and finger. "I can't do any of that, because our parents are married, which means by law, you're my sister. And brothers aren't allowed to watch their sisters touch themselves. Brothers aren't allowed to suck their sister's cunts. And brothers definitely aren't allowed to fuck their sisters on a bearskin rug in front of a fireplace."

I squirmed, warmth spreading between my legs at his words. "I don't care," I gasped. "We're not related by blood. We didn't grow up together. We just met. Pretend I'm someone you picked up at a bar."

He smiled and squeezed my nipple between his thumb and forefinger until I whimpered with longing. "The problem with that," he said slowly, "Is that you gotta pass muster with all three of us."

"I can do that," I said, fisting his t-shirt in my hand.

He pulled the cup of my bra back into place, then trailed his knuckles down my belly, drawing a slow circle around my bellybutton. "That's what I'm afraid of."

His breath whispered across my cheek, and the woodsy smell of him intoxicated me. Nerves tingled all through my body, increasing the wetness pooling between my legs.

"I better go," he whispered, his dark eyes fixed on my lips.

"Wait," I whispered. "Not yet."

He raised his eyebrows, waiting.

"Tell me more," I said.

"You like it when I talk dirty?" he asked, a smile tugging at the corner of his mouth.

I nodded, biting my lip but not looking away.

A soft whisper of a laugh escaped him. He reached up and rested his fingers under my chin, tugging my lip free of my teeth. "You really think you could handle all three of us?"

"I know I can."

But I wasn't so sure. I'd felt the size of both his brothers, and I didn't think half of one of them could fit inside me.

His thumb caressed my lower lip, rolling it down and smearing the wetness from inside over both my lips. When my lips were wet, he rested his thumb against the center of my lower lip.

A shiver of longing coursed through me.

"I don't think you could handle a single one of us," he said. His thumb pressed harder, parting my lips, slipping between my teeth. He gripped my jaw and eased my mouth open, his thumb pinning my tongue down. I could do nothing but close my lips around his thumb. I bit down gently, trapping his thumb. When he didn't pull back, I let my tongue curl around his thumb, wetting it as I began to suck gently. His eyes widened for half a second, then locked on my lips. I sucked harder, harder, imagining how hard his cock must be inside his jeans right now.

Suddenly, his grip clamped down on my jaw, his thumb crushing my tongue. My mouth opened automatically, and he drew his thumb out. He wiped it dry on his t-shirt, dark amusement in his eyes. "You do that to a guy, you'll give him a second circumcision," he said, patting my cheek. "But nice try, Princess."

With that, he threw the blanket off, hopped to his feet, and strolled out of the room while I lay there, my face an inferno.

TEN

Amber

"What am I going to do?" I moaned over the phone to Haley after I told her the latest development with the guys—and their mother.

"I can send you another finger vibe," she said.

"Seriously, though, what would you do?"

Haley laughed. "You're talking to the girl who went around high school telling everyone that I was taking back the power of the word *slut* by proudly claiming it."

"But what about their mother?" I asked.

"Fuck their mother," she said. "She sounds like the kind of woman who thinks sex is a woman's duty to her country so she can make more sons. That's what she did, right?"

"Yeah, but it doesn't solve my problem, unless you think she wants me to get knocked up by all her sons."

"I don't know what you want me to say,"

Haley said. "If you want to stay in your room and hide from them for two months, I'll email you some porn."

"I might need some," I said. "But strictly for instructional purposes. Waylon thought I was trying to circumcise his thumb when I sucked on it sexily."

Haley howled with laughter. "I guess it's good you started with a thumb," she said at last.

"Yeah, I don't really want to swallow a foreskin," I said. "No matter how hot the owner is."

"I just threw up in my mouth."

This time, I nearly died laughing. Which was better than dying of shame, as I was pretty sure I'd almost done after Waylon's comment. How dare that bastard make fun of my inexperience? It wasn't like I was a virgin by choice. Okay, I'd chosen to stay with Charlie, but seriously, I'd have felt like the shallowest bitch on earth if I'd dumped a guy for not hooking up. After all, a guy couldn't dump a girl for not hooking up, not without being called a disgusting pig.

Now, more than ever, I regretted those wasted years. I could have been out screwing my way through all the boys in Manhattan. I'd know exactly how to suck on a guy's thumb to make him come in his pants and beg me to move on to his cock, instead of patting my cheek like I was his virginal little sister. And I'd probably be nice and loose so I could fit all three of their enormous penises inside me at the same time. Hell, babies would just drop out of me one after another, and their mother would be happy, too.

"Seriously, Amber, you can't hide out in your room for the next two months."

"Like hell I can't," I said. "They're pigs and they don't deserve me."

"No one deserves you," Haley said. "Except me, and I'm not really into eating pussy, no offense. But I do know you pretty well, and I don't think hiding in shame is what you really want to do."

"It's not," I said, throwing myself back on my pillows. "What I want is for my mom not to be married to their dad so they'll stop trying to push me away. Do you think we can break them up?"

Haley laughed. "Not in two months."

"Hmm, okay. What about getting them used to the idea so they'll give us their blessing? You think we could do that in two months?"

"Not even in two million years," Haley said. "Look, Amber, if you start hooking up with even one of your stepbrothers, people are going to freak out. And if you're hooking up with all of them, they'll completely lose their shit. I'm not going to lie. That's what'll happen. So the question is, are you willing to risk that? Or not?"

ELEVEN

Sawyer

"You were up late last night," Holden said to Waylon at breakfast. His voice was bland, but I knew he was up to something, the way a brother just knows.

Waylon paused, then shoveled a forkful of eggs into his mouth. "Storm," he muttered.

I took a long swig of coffee before wading it. "You could call her that."

Waylon glanced up and then continued eating.

"Look, we've been waiting for the right woman for three goddamn years," I said. "I'm tired of waiting. She's the first woman who's ever come close to what we're looking for."

"And here she is, delivered to our doorstep," Holden said. "That's gotta be a sign."

Waylon grunted.

"I say we give her a chance," I said. "If she wants to, of course."

"Oh, she wants to," Waylon said.

"And what other woman has wanted to, not run screaming from the idea, and not just treated it like one wild night?" I asked.

"Even if Dad did marry her mom, we're all adults now," Holden said. "It's unfortunate, but it can't be helped. That's not our fault. And it's not hers. And we never even lived together as stepsiblings. It's not weird."

Waylon snorted. "Tell that to the people in town," he said. "Tell it to our parents."

"They may not be thrilled, but they can't do shit about it," I reminded him. "When else will we have a woman like her? She's perfect, she's willing, she's open-minded..." Not to mention she made my cock stiff every time she touched me. But I didn't have to tell them that—I knew they felt it, too. I could see the strain of restraint on them every time she walked in the room, same as it was for me.

"I'll agree with one thing," Waylon said. "It's time the old man learned he can't control us anymore. He's been doing it all our lives. Even now, dangling a loan over our heads. Making us take care of Amber. We'll take care of her all right."

"You in agreement, then?" Holden asked, watching our big brother intently.

"I didn't say that," Waylon said, setting down his fork and taking a gulp of coffee. "We can't have it getting out that we're all living up here and in a relationship. And it will get out. Eventually, it will. Just like it got out with Maria—and that time, it wasn't even the truth."

"We can protect her better if she's on the inside with us," I said. "She's trouble, I'll admit. But I always did like trouble."

"She's got more to lose than we do," Waylon said. "She's still a teenager, for Christ's sake. She may not understand it now, but it could ruin her entire professional life, something like that getting into the news."

"Protecting her comes first," Holden agreed. "We'll have to make sure nothing gets out that could tarnish her reputation. It should be her choice."

"We gotta do what's right for us, too," I said. "And what I see in her, it's right for you both. It's about time we had a woman we could all love. And one who respects and cares for our needs, too." All I could think about was how eager she'd been to kiss me at the table the other day, how willing she was. I didn't think we'd get any hesitation on her part. If we put the question to her, we had to be pretty damn sure she'd accept. And it seemed we were.

Waylon got up and picked up his hat, pushing it low on his head. "I don't think I can resist her much longer, anyway," he growled "She's like a cat in heat."

"I was just thinking the same thing," I said, standing and downing the rest of my coffee, chewing the stray grounds between my teeth as I grabbed my own hat and coat.

"We can't just go in there cocks blazing,"

Waylon said. "Not if she's a damn virgin."

"Fuck, I forgot about that," I said. "She can't be. She doesn't act like one."

"She acts like one to me," Waylon said.

"I thought she was a party girl in New York," Holden added. "And she was drunk when she said that. Surely she didn't mean it…"

I set my cup in the sink and turned back to my brothers. "Only one way to find out for sure."

TWELVE

Amber

November began white as Christmas. Snow fell during the night, piling up on what was left of the last one. I spent my days avoiding the Grimeses and taking care of the horses, and my nights chatting with Haley and ordering decorations for the house.

A few days after the wine debacle, as Holden was clearing the dinner dishes, Sawyer smiled across the table at me. "Feel like a nightcap?"

I didn't, mostly because I was afraid I'd end up making an ass of myself again, but the mischievous light in his eyes made me hesitate. When he yawned hugely and stretched his arms over his head, I caved. Seriously, those arms would be my undoing.

"Maybe, for a minute," I said, keenly aware of Waylon's silent, watchful presence at the head of the table.

"We just want to talk," Holden said, rinsing a plate and setting it in the dishwasher.

"It didn't seem like dinner table conversation," Sawyer said with that mischievous smile.

"What does that mean?" I asked, cocking an eyebrow at him.

Instead of answering, he took a bottle of whiskey from atop the fridge and opened the cabinet to retrieve four whiskey glasses. "Can you handle whiskey?" he asked, a challenge in his voice.

"Oh, I can handle whiskey," I said. "I'm a Manhattan girl, remember?"

"Apparently not wine, though," Waylon rumbled from the end of the table. He was frowning at me.

I just fixed him with my sweetest smile. "It's not the whiskey you should be worried about."

"It's not," he said, his voice low and steady, his eyes fixed on mine. A shiver went through me. I could never tell if he wanted to rip my clothes off or rip my face off.

After my brief slips with the other two, things had gone back to normal. But Waylon had never been the same since the night he saw me naked. It wasn't like I meant to fall in the cow water when it was thirty degrees outside. I didn't know why he held that against me. It had been his idea to take all my wet clothes off.

Sawyer stepped between us, breaking the tension crackling in the air. He set the glasses down and neatly poured a bit into each.

"Don't tell anyone I'm serving alcohol to a minor," he said with a wink.

"Ha," I said. "Just because I'm not twenty-one doesn't mean I'm underage."

"Uh huh," Waylon said.

"Trust me, I've had a fake ID for a while, and it was not going to waste."

"That, or Daddy has a liquor cabinet," he said.

I tried to hide the sting of that, because it was true. I had raided Dad's liquor cabinet on more than one occasion when I'd started wanting to try things I shouldn't. But Waylon's insinuating that I was a liar made my blood boil. Plus, I didn't like thinking of Dad not being married to Mom, because their dad was. It was too creepy.

"Let's take this in the other room," Sawyer said, picking up a glass and heading for the living room. The rest of us followed, silence weighing heavy in the air.

Holden sat on one end of the leather couch. Sawyer steered me towards the couch, his hand on the small of my back. "Have a seat, Princess," he said.

I took a seat next to Holden, suddenly feeling like I was about to be handed my walking papers. Were they sending me back to New York? Had I crossed a line with Waylon that was okay to cross with the others, but not with him?

I threw back my whiskey like a shot before turning to face Waylon, who had taken the armchair instead of joining us on the couch.

"Slow down, there, Princess," Sawyer said, sloshing a little more whiskey into my glass before sitting on my other side.

"We have something to talk to you about," Waylon said, glowering from under the brim of his hat, which was pulled low over his dark eyes like usual.

"Please don't tell me you're sending me to live with your mother," I blurted out.

"We told you we weren't," Holden said. "You can trust us, Amber. We wouldn't do that."

I gulped again at his intense, serious expression. All I could do was nod mutely, though I wanted to slide over and snuggle into his safe arms. This wasn't the time.

"It's more of a proposal," Sawyer said, excitement radiating through his smile. It washed over me, and a tingle of anticipation crept into my nervousness.

"An indecent proposal?" I asked, unable to keep myself from smiling back at him.

"The most indecent," he said. "But we wanted to clear up some things first. Make sure we're all on the same page."

"All?" I asked, remembering Waylon there, glowering at me.

"I guess you've probably gotten the idea we all want to fuck you," Sawyer said, sipping his whiskey.

I nearly coughed whiskey all over him.

Like that was just a normal thing to say!

But then, I always had liked his candor. He didn't make me wonder, unlike some people. Some people named Waylon.

I swallowed my mouthful of whiskey so fast my eyes burned. "Right now?"

"Not right now," Waylon growled, sounding irritated.

"I don't know," Sawyer said, looking me over in a way that made those tingles of excitement take root between my legs. "I'd give it a whirl."

I set my glass down so I wouldn't finish it off before they'd finished one. Now was not the time to get sloppy drunk and make an ass of myself, either. Not when three men had just told me they wanted to fuck me. All of them.

Suddenly, my head was spinning.

Holden reached out and took my hand. "Amber, we're not holding you hostage. We just want to clear the air. Put everything out there."

I nodded. I'd never been around guys like this, who just came out and said that without preamble, so matter-of-factly. Of course, most of the guys I'd been around were still in fucking high school, or at bars, so they were all about the games.

"That doesn't mean you have to want us back," Holden said. "Sawyer just means that we all like you. So there it is. We want you to know. And we wouldn't mind knowing how you feel. If there's one of us you'd like to pursue a relationship with, we'll all protect you both."

"Protect me?"

"From prying eyes, wagging tongues…" Sawyer said, then added a wink. "Except ours, of course."

"If anyone finds out, it won't be just gossip," Waylon said. "It could ruin your reputation, and not just around here."

I imagined it now. The tabloids. The scandal I was supposed to be escaping. My mother's career. Their father's career.

Manhattan Socialite Deflowered by Three Sexy Cowboys in Wyoming Home

Just Breaking: Sexy Cherry-Popping Cowboys Manhattan Socialite's Stepbrothers

"And our parents' careers," I said, my heart throbbing in my chest.

"Then we'll just have to make sure no one finds out," Sawyer said.

For a minute, we all just sat in silence. Finally Sawyer shifted and crossed his foot over his knee.

"No matter who you choose, we're all behind you, one hundred percent," Holden said.

I realized then that they were waiting for an answer. I had to pick.

Forgetting my reservations, I gulped down a swallow of burning whiskey, then set my glass down and wiped my hands on my jeans. Well, this was just craptastic. How was I supposed to choose?

THIRTEEN

Amber

My eyes moved over Holden, his massive thighs and the bulge in his jeans. I swallowed and let my eyes continue up his body to his bulging arms that I wanted wrapped around me all night, his broad shoulders and thick chest, and his serious face. Those warm brown eyes, his soft lips, his sweet manner. His concern for me, his artistic side, the way he'd used me as his muse. He was the safe choice, and I'd break his heart if I didn't want him. How could I not choose him?

But then there was Sawyer. Blunt, yes, but fun and straightforward. No games. He wanted me, and I wanted him. We could cook together, flirt and share food. I had fantasized about him throwing me down on the kitchen table more than once. And he was just as sexy as Holden, with those arms that made me positively drool. Between that and his blonde hair and the stubble on his cheeks, that sexy wink of his that made me feel like I was in on all his jokes, and his mischievous smile that always reached his blue eyes, how could I pick anyone else?

And then there was Waylon. I was pretty sure he was the one I shouldn't choose. But that only made me want to choose him more. I'd only barely gotten to know him, a rare glimpse once in a while, even as I felt like I was getting to know the others pretty well now. Waylon was the standoffish one, the watcher. He made me feel like an idiot most of the time, and I didn't know exactly how he'd take rejection. Hell, I wasn't even sure he wanted me at all, despite our little fireside chat.

He was the boss, though. I could just tell. And I could imagine what it would be like for him to boss me around between the sheets. The thought of it both excited and scared me a little. But in a good way.

Basically, I wanted them all. So yeah, maybe I was a greedy bitch.

"I...I can't," I said, wanting nothing more than to run from the room. But they'd been straight with me, so I owed it to them to be straight with them.

"Why not?" Waylon asked.

"I'm sorry," I said, staring at the coffee table, wishing I had more to drink. That had always been my surest bet, my escape. But now I was stone cold sober and itching to drown my reality in a bottle.

"Don't be sorry," Holden said. "There's no blame here. We understand."

"No, it's not that I don't like you," I said quickly. "I mean, I like you a lot. All of you." I gulped, trying to slow the torrent of nervous words building inside me. But as usual, it overtook my sense of reason, and all came pouring out. I was shit at keeping my feelings to myself. "But that's just it. I'm sorry. I can't pick one of you, because I'm just getting to know you, and I really don't know who I like more, because you're all equally yummy, if we're being honest. Don't make me choose. It's too much pressure. See, I like all of you for different reasons, and together, you make the world's most perfect, hottest guy. But individually—I mean, I'm not saying that any of you are less than perfect, but—"

"It's okay," Sawyer said, looking infuriatingly amused. "Nobody's perfect."

"Yeah, I mean, look at me. I take verbal diarrhea to new heights."

Did I just say diarrhea *in front of the three hottest guys on the planet?*

"Is that what you call it?" Waylon said, sounding less amused.

"I'm sorry," I said. "I can't choose."

"I thought as much," Waylon said.

"We were hoping you'd say that," Sawyer said. He had that delighted smile shining all over his face again.

I gulped. "You were? Why?"

"Because we all like you, too," Holden said, like that explained everything.

"And you didn't want me to choose one of you and hurt the other two? I don't get it."

"No," Sawyer said, scooting closer and angling himself to face me on the couch. "We wanted to make sure before we opened ourselves up to you."

"Okay…"

"See, we've been waiting a long time for the right woman to come along," he said. "One who understood what kind of lifestyle we want, and who might be open to seeing how it goes."

"I'm afraid I'm a little lost," I said. "What's this lifestyle?"

"We want to share."

I remembered their words to me before. *We share everything.* Hadn't they all said that to me now, at one point or another.

"Share…me?" I asked, just to make sure.

"Exactly," Sawyer said.

I'd thought about it. Of course I had. I'd fantasized about it. They'd even hinted at it before. But now that it was all out in the open, staring me in the face, I didn't know. A fantasy was one thing. Reality was another. How was I, a senator's virginal daughter, going to handle three big burly cowboys? How could I keep them satisfied? I'd never even seen a real life penis, let alone had three of them stuffed inside me at once.

"How would it work?" I asked at last, after a long silence.

"However you want it to work," Holden said,

taking my hand again. "You're in complete control. You don't have to do anything you don't want to do, ever. We'll respect your boundaries."

"Do we need, like, a schedule? A safe word?"

"No schedule," Holden said. "Just whatever you're in the mood for."

Sawyer grinned. "And you don't need a safe word. Just tell us what you want and don't want. We're not planning on tying you up and gagging you. Unless, of course, you're into that."

"I might be," I said, giving him my most charming grin. But of course I was faking. I was full of shit. I had no idea what I was into.

Waylon cleared his throat and shifted in his armchair. Of course it was Waylon who saw through me. "You told our mother you were a virgin," he reminded me.

"Okay, so I may not have had an actual penis inside me, but I'm quite adept with a vibrator," I offered.

"Christ." He leaned his head back and closed his eyes like I was trying his patience.

"Well, it's not like I meant to be a virgin," I said. "I had a boyfriend for a long time, but he said he was celibate. He was basically a human chastity belt. Hell, for all I know, my parents hired him to be my boyfriend so I wouldn't run around sleeping with anyone they didn't pre-approve. And then I found him getting busy with two other girls, and I threw soup on him, and eggs, and he called the cops on me.

And that's how I got arrested and ended up here."

There was a long moment of silence. "That's why you got arrested?" Holden asked.

I nodded, my throat suddenly tight. I didn't want to think about that asshole cheating on me, about how much I'd trusted him and what a sucker I'd been. It wasn't fair for Waylon to blame me for that. Suddenly, I had the horrifying realization that I was about to burst into tears.

"Who is this guy?" Sawyer said. "I think he needs a taste of Wyoming justice."

"No, it's fine," I said, taking a shaky breath. "I'm over it. I just want to get on with my life. That's part of why I came out here. To get away from that whole mess."

"You should have told us," Holden said quietly. "We wouldn't be putting this on you if we knew that's what you just went through."

His kindness just made me want to cry more. But I wasn't going to cry on them about Charlie. He didn't deserve my tears, and these guys deserved much more.

"I don't want to be treated with kid gloves," I said. "I'm not broken. And I'm tired of being treated like a fragile artifact kept behind bulletproof glass. I don't want to be seen and not touched."

"Oh, we won't put you on a shelf," Waylon said, lifting his head. "If we do this, if you want a relationship with all three of us, we'll do more than touch you."

I shivered at the thought.

He sat forward, his hands knotting between his knees. "Don't get me wrong. We'll admire you. But it won't be from afar. We're going to fuck you, Amber. All of us."

God, all three of them! What if it was too many?

"But if you're that inexperienced...we're going to have to get you ready for it before we go there. Train you a little."

"Train me?" I asked, anger erasing my urge to cry. "I'm not a dog."

"No," he said. "You're a virgin. And a virgin can't handle what we're going to do to you."

"Oh," I said, swallowing past the anticipation building inside me. "What exactly does that entail?"

"Oh, you'll see," Waylon said. "We might even give you a taste of it tonight."

"Tonight?" The thought made me breathless, and I could feel pressure building between my legs.

"Are you in?" Sawyer asked eagerly. "Is this really what you want? All three of us, together and apart?"

I nodded again, quivering with excitement at the prospect of three men wanting me. Not the way Charlie did, as an arm piece and a political move. They just flat out wanted me. And I wanted them. "I'm in."

"This isn't a one-night thing," Holden said. "We're not talking about a foursome. We're talking about a relationship. All of us being together. Maybe for a long time. We don't just want to claim your body, Amber. We want your heart and soul to belong to us, too."

I almost told them it already did. But it seemed awfully soon to be talking about love.

"You realize if there's gossip, people will be harsher to you," Waylon warned.

I remembered my mother telling me to grow up, that I should know life wasn't fair. Well, she sure had picked a good place to send me. I was about to do all kinds of growing up.

"The three of us will do everything we can to protect you from that, and make sure it doesn't happen," Sawyer said. "If we don't react to the idle gossip, it'll go away. And if we don't feed it, it won't come back."

I thought of Mrs. Grimes out there in her cabin, nosing around or peering through the window.

"Then we'll be careful," I said. "But I want to do this. With all of you."

I still couldn't believe they were okay with sharing. I kept waiting for the punchline, or to wake up from this dream. I'd gone from a guy who wouldn't even touch my boobs to three guys who looked like they had their hearts set on devouring every inch of me.

"So," Sawyer said, draping his arm across my the back of the couch. "How about that taste we mentioned earlier?"

FOURTEEN

Amber

I gulped. "A...taste?"

Sawyer's eyes flicked down and then back up, and he grinned. "Yeah. Just a sample of what's to come. For all four of us."

"Okay," I whispered, my heart hammering.

Holden scooted closer on my other side. "Don't worry," he said, his muscular arm sliding around me and pulling me close. "You don't have to do anything you're not ready for."

I gulped. If I was going to do this, I might as well do it all the way. I was so fucking ready. "Okay," I said. "What do I need to do?"

"Just relax and enjoy," Sawyer said with a wink.

Holden massaged my shoulder, his eyes serious. "The second you want to stop, just say the word and we'll stop, no questions asked."

"No safe word?"

"How about *stop?*" Sawyer asked. "Just tell us, and we'll stop. Relax, Princess. We're all adults here. We can control ourselves."

I looked up at Waylon, who had moved to stand beside the fire, his face blank as a statue's. I had to work harder to read him, studying his dark eyes. The rest of his face gave nothing away. "Who goes first?" I asked.

The other brothers looked to Waylon, too.

"That's your call, Princess," he said.

Craptastic. I didn't want to decide that. I'd never even been naked in front of a guy. And now these three gorgeous men who all had experiences beyond my imaginings were asking me to choose what I wanted.

"I's okay, Am," Holden said, turning my face towards him. "We can just play it by ear."

I'd thought Waylon would step in and take control, claim me first because he was oldest. But he only stood at the fire, watching as Holden's lips skimmed over mine. Sawyer scooted closer, but he didn't touch me.

My heart skipped as Holden's lips claimed mine again, more firmly this time. He shifted his position, kneeling between my knees. This was it. My heart skipped in my chest, but Holden tugged me forward, kissing my lips again. His tongue pressed between my lips, sweeping over mine. Suddenly, I couldn't wait. Warmth built between my legs, pressure and anticipation flooding through me as his tongue tasted mine. I could just imagine how it would feel between my other lips.

Soon, his mouth moved to my ear, and shivers ran through my body. I grabbed his shoulders, massaging those gorgeous muscles. "Now," I whispered, closing my eyes and leaning back on the couch.

Holden slid down, undoing the button of my jeans. I lifted my hips, and he slid them down. Air blew across my bare skin, and I was suddenly aware how naked I was. They were all dressed, and I was now only wearing a shirt. This was really happening.

I opened my eyes. Holden was staring at my pussy like it was the Mona Lisa, the world's biggest ruby, and a t-bone steak combined. Which made for a weird picture, but hey, he was an artist, he could probably pull it off.

I watched as he slowly lowered himself to reach me. His huge hands moved up me, holding my waist as he lowered his mouth between my thighs. A wave of desire washed over me, and I parted my knees for him. His tongue slid between my lips. With one long, slow stroke, he erased my untouched status. I was lost in the sensation of his hot, wet tongue so thoroughly tasting what had never been so much as seen by a man before.

Now three sets of eyes had seen my most private, intimate spot.

Holden bent low again, his hands moving up to cup my breasts, his fingers firm but gentle. His wide, wet tongue started at my ass and in another stroke, moved all the way to my clit. I gasped as he swiped across my sensitive spot. My clit throbbed against his tongue and he moaned, pulsing his tongue against it.

Beside me, Sawyer shifted, stroking himself as he watched his brother's tongue take its time with the third pass. Holden bent one more time, spreading the folds open as he slowly dragged his tongue through my wetness to my swollen clit. I leaned my head back and lifted my hips, wanting more, needing him to linger on my clit, give it a little more love and attention. The pressure was unbearable.

He sat back and licked his lips. "Thank you," he said, then climbed to his feet.

Thank you? Did guys normally thank girls for the first taste of their cherry? For being the first tongue to ever explore me?

But none of this was normal. These men were the first to lay eyes on me, but I couldn't say who was first. They'd all seen me at once.

They'd be the first to touch me, to explore me and taste me and fuck me, the first to come inside me and make me come. And the law said they were my brothers.

"I—can I go freshen up?" I asked.

"Of course," Sawyer said with a grin. "Don't take too long, though. I'm dying for a taste of that sweet pussy."

I wasn't sure if I should put my pants back

on, but it seemed pointless, so I just stepped over them and into the bathroom. I'd said I wanted all this and more. A relationship, all of them, for a long time. But could I do it?

My body said it could handle it. My pussy throbbed with longing, aching to be filled. It felt swollen as I splashed a little water over it, cleaning it for Sawyer. Holden had definitely gotten a taste. I didn't know what was left for the others. Maybe rinsing off between them would be enough to make them all feel like they were getting something new, instead of just tasting each other.

I patted myself dry and headed back out, feeling awkward without pants. But Sawyer erased that in a second, striding over to meet me halfway to the couch and sweeping me into his arms. He kissed me passionately, his tongue driving between my lips and claiming mine. My toes skimmed the floor as he carried me around the couch and knelt, setting me back in my spot. With a grin, he grabbed my ass and pulled me forward, to the very edge of the couch.

"Lay back and enjoy the show, Princess," he said.

"Get her a pillow," Waylon said, his voice flat and commanding, without emotion. He hadn't moved since we'd started, and still stood by the fireplace with his arms crossed. I swallowed, suddenly feeling as exposed as if I were naked and spread eagle before him. Which was only halfway the case.

Holden pushed a couple pillows behind me.

Still cupping my ass in his hands, Sawyer lowered his head. But instead of going for broke like Holden had, his teasing lips met my hipbone. I could see the smile in the corner of his lips as he flicked out his tongue and wiggled it against my bare skin. I gasped at the spasm of ticklishness that went through me. Sawyer did it again, until I started giggling helplessly. Then his lips moved across my belly to my belly button, which he flicked his tongue inside. He sat back, grinning, and tugged at the bottom of my shirt.

"What happened to just a taste?" I teased.

"Sorry," Sawyer said, not looking at all sorry. "Can I taste your nipples?"

I laughed. "Aren't you greedy?"

"Not tonight," Waylon said. "That wasn't what we promised."

I didn't know what they'd promised, but for some reason, a tiny wash of relief went through me. Being completely naked before all three of them, when they were fully clothed, was too much. I'd never even kissed Waylon, but I could have kissed him then. Maybe all that quiet, detached observing was there for a reason. It kept me safe to have him watching so closely, picking up on my signals.

"You're right," Sawyer said. "We've got plenty of time for that. I'm not in a hurry."

With that, he scooted back on his knees and bent, still cupping my ass. He nosed my legs apart and kissed my mound, then my clit. I arched up, having expected him to do as Holden did. Instead, his lips caressed my clit, kissing it and tugging it gently. I sucked in a breath, then stifled a cry when the tip of his tongue flicked out and swiped the sensitive tip.

The tension that had built when Holden licked me began to rise again, and that need to be filled, that unbearable cry for release, gripped my body. Sawyer's tongue made a slow circle around my clit, as if winding me tighter. My fingers clenched in his hair, and I thought I was going to break at any moment, to say I couldn't take it. I could feel myself growing wetter and wetter as Sawyer's tongue squirmed lower, tasting my juices.

The tip of his tongue flicked against my opening and I cried out, arching up, unable to control my body. It wanted to be filled, satisfied. I needed release, not to be teased with the tip of a tongue. I needed to be fucked hard with his thick cock.

"That's enough," I heard Waylon growl.

I opened my eyes, bewildered. I'd forgotten where I was, who I was, who was watching Sawyer eat me so thoroughly, so wonderfully. Holden's eyes were riveted between my legs, but Waylon was watching my face. His eyes burned with lust, so dark and it made me shiver. Sawyer's lips closed around my clit and he gave one quick suck.

I cried out again, grasping his head, wanting to keep him there. But he pulled away and gave me a wicked grin. "Next time, Princess."

Were they serious? They were going to push

me to the brink and leave me unsatisfied? Was that what they'd meant by just a taste? I just got a preview, but no relief?

Before I could protest, Sawyer had stood and Waylon took his place. He grabbed me and lifted me up, off the couch. With one arm, he swept everything off the coffee table. Empty whiskey glasses and magazines tumbled across the hardwood. Waylon laid me down on the coffee table, his eyes fierce and dark as hell. A shiver of raw lust trembled my thighs as he knelt over me. Was he going to fuck me?

God, I wouldn't say no. I wanted it, needed it, his huge cock to fill me to the brim and break me wide open.

I gripped the edges of the table, my whole body wracked with shivers of longing.

Waylon gripped my knees and spread them wide, as wide as they'd go. I remembered then that I hadn't washed up, that I was spread open and glistening with my own wetness and that of Sawyer's tongue. But I didn't care. I needed to be fucked.

Waylon released one of my knees. He licked his thumb, then gently circled it around my clit, not touching the sensitive, swollen tip. He slid his thumb through my wetness and covered my opening. I began to squirm, trying to get him to push it inside me.

"Hold still," Waylon said, removing his thumb and licking it. Was that the taste he wanted?

"Fuck me," I whispered.

FIFTEEN

Amber

Waylon's eyes were burning as he pushed my knees open again. Sawyer gripped one of them, pulling my legs wide so he could see while his other hand undid his fly. He pulled out his cock, huge and naked, and a shiver of longing and terror ran straight down my spine. I wasn't big enough for half his cock, let alone the whole thing.

Waylon nodded at my other knee, and Holden slipped around to hold it, his grip gentle behind my knee. He licked his lips, watching my pussy spread further open that it had been for him.

"I need it," I gasped. "Fuck me, Waylon."

He tore his eyes from mine, raking them down my body, then buried his face between my legs. There was no preparation like Holden, no teasing like Sawyer. His tongue swiped through my wetness, then plunged into my opening. I cried out in surprise as he sucked, drinking me down, then thrust his tongue inside me again, tunneling deeper this time. The pressure mounted, winding painfully tight. I tried to clamp my legs around his head, but the other two held them open.

"Oh God, fuck me," I moaned.

Waylon's tongue punched into me again and again, fucking me. Pushing me closer to an edge I knew I could never go back from once I stepped over. And I didn't want to.

I looked up at Holden, whose eyes were hooded with lust, and Sawyer, who was running his hand up and down his huge cock. Not my brothers, but my partners in this. Waylon's tongue drove deeper, until his nose was flattened against my pelvic bone and his teeth pressing into my flesh. I cried out and I grabbed onto the other two, Sawyer's shoulder and Holden's free hand, to anchor myself.

Waylon's tongue tasted me, drank me, opened me where no man ever had. It went faster and faster until I couldn't take it another second. The tension was unbearable. I arched up, letting go of the others and grabbing his head. I buried it between my legs, grinding myself against his face. I moaned, then cried out. His tongue filled me, and body went rigid, my walls tightening around his tongue until all at once something split. I screamed, waves of ecstasy washing over me with each pulse of my cunt around his tongue. Arching up, I drowned him in my juices, his tongue wriggling to gain my depths.

He pulled away slowly, gave one last suck to

my throbbing opening, and sat back on the heels of his cowboy boots.

"Can they have one more taste?" he asked.

"Please," Sawyer groaned. "I'm dying here, Princess."

I didn't realize what he was asking until Holden took my hand and squeezed. "It's okay if you don't want us to. But I want to taste your come."

I couldn't seem to form words, but I nodded mutely, my mind reeling with the intense but matter-of-fact way he'd just asked what sounded like a very dirty proposition.

Sawyer moved around my knee and bent down, swiping his tongue through my wetness and moaning as he sucked away my juices. My clit throbbed, and I could feel his body tense and jerk for several seconds. He lay his head on my stomach, breathing hard.

After a minute, he got up and disappeared into the bathroom. Holden squeezed my hand once before slipping between my knees.

He bent and slowly tasted me, his lips and tongue exploring me more thoroughly this time. He sucked gently at my clit, then slid his tongue through my wetness and dipped it into my opening. He sucked once, then lapped up the juices between my lips, on my ass and thighs. By the time he was done, that coil of desire was rebuilding inside me. I knew I'd need release again soon. At last, Holden sat up. "You tasted amazing before," he said. "But you taste even better now."

When he stood, I felt more naked than I'd ever felt. I'd just come, screaming, in front of three men while they all watched. I'd let them hold me open while Waylon tongue-fucked me until I was helpless to stop screaming with pleasure. Now I was lying on the coffee table with my sex naked, open, wrecked.

Waylon moved over to me and draped the blanket from the couch over me as if I were something obscene. I figured they'd both go up to their rooms to jerk off and let me get dressed. But Waylon scooped me up and carried me to the couch, where he sat, pulling me down onto his lap.

"Was that too much?" he asked.

"Yes," I panted, still out of breath. "But no."

For the first time, a genuine smile tugged at the corners of his lips. "This is just the beginning," he said. "Now that you've had a taste, are you still on board for being in a relationship with three men?"

"Waylon Westling," I said. "Are you propositioning me?"

"Didn't I already do that?"

"Usually you let the others do the talking."

"They're better at it," he said, looking away.

For the first time, I realized maybe his silence wasn't arrogance. Could he be self-conscious about something? Waylon, this impenetrable mountain of steel?

"I think you're pretty good at it," I said,

snuggling closer to his chest. "You talked to me by the fire that night."

He made a soft, snorting noise but didn't answer. After a minute, his arms tightened around me, and he kissed my hair. I realized then that he'd had his tongue deeper inside me than I'd ever had anything, except maybe my own finger, but he'd never even kissed my lips. The thought made my face burn for a second, but it quickly turned to a sense of naughtiness.

I'd never thought of myself as someone who wanted to feel dirty and wild, but maybe I did. I had fantasies, but I'd never shared them with Charlie, of course. He would have shamed me I played at being a bad girl, but I was only the closely regulated version of one that Charlie allowed. He made the rules not only about how far we could go, but how far *I* could go, how wild I could be.

I could party and get drunk and puke out the door of a cab, I could put my leg behind my head in front of an entire bar. And Charlie was cool, he wasn't jealous. He'd laugh along with everyone else. He'd let me dance with other men. I'd even kissed other men when I was wasted, though I didn't remember it. He'd told me. And he'd forgiven me. But I'd felt like dirt for it. It hadn't been my choice, really, but because I was out of control drunk and horny as hell.

Now here I was, in full control of myself. And in control of how far not just I went, not just my boyfriend, but three men. I set the rules here. I made the boundaries, not them. I was the one in power. And I could be as dirty as I wanted to be.

If I had fantasies, no matter what they were, I felt safe to share them without judgment. After all, they had opened themselves and shared their deepest wish with me. I hadn't judged them, hadn't run. And when I shared mine, I knew at least one of the guys would be eager to fulfill them—if not all of them. I could have any of them, or all of them, or none of them, whenever I wanted. I had choices. But why choose?

It was hard to think beyond basic sex when you couldn't have anything. Now the world had opened before me. I felt like I was becoming a new person, at least sexually. I was blossoming. I could be anyone I wanted, as wild or as chaste as I chose. I set the pace. I made the rules.

I lifted my face to Waylon. "Kiss me," I whispered.

And he did.

SIXTEEN

Amber

The next day, I asked Grimes to saddle up Van Gogh so I could ride. I stood back watching him work, trying to memorize everything he was doing. I'd seen Holden do it before, and it didn't look too hard. If I could lift it, I could probably saddle her up myself.

As usual, Grimes didn't say a word, but he gave me creepy looks every now and then, eyeing my body like a dog watching meat marinating on the counter. Since I was wearing a scarf and a puffy yellow down jacket, his lusty looks were either a testament to how little he was getting from his wife or how much marshmallow Peeps turned him on.

When he finished saddling the horse, I took the reins and led her out, trying not to notice his eyes slithering down my legs as I passed him. Outside, I shoved my foot in the stirrup, grabbed the saddle horn, and hoisted myself up. I threw my leg over Van Gogh, got myself settled into the saddle, and gave the horse a gentle squeeze with my knees, shaking the reigns to encourage her. Relieved to be away from Grimes, I let my hood fall back and the chilly wind whip through my hair, searing my cheeks.

It felt good to be out in the fresh air, in all that wide open space. I realized as I rode that all that emptiness around me didn't feel weird anymore, like I'd hurtle off the earth because there was nothing to hold onto. When I'd first come to Wyoming, it had seemed too big, but now, as the horse began to trot, I realized that I loved all that space. Space to run the horses, to move the cows from one pasture to the next. Space to run away and think when I needed to.

If I was living with three guys, there were bound to be days when I needed my space. As much as I desired and adored them, I liked my own time, too. It might get exhausting to be wanted by three men all the time. I tried to imagine the four of us crammed up in some tiny New York apartment. It just wouldn't do.

But out here...out here, I could ride away on Van Gogh, have space to breathe. And it wasn't really empty space, like I'd thought when I arrived. There was lots here—the aspens along the edge of the property, fences dividing it, a creek, grass, bits of snow in the shade, fields, feeders, barns, hay bales, watering tanks, ponds, farm equipment, the little cabins...

In a way, the place had as much going on as New York. It was just a lot lower here, except for the mountains in the distance.

I wondered if the guys ever visited their dad in New York. I couldn't imagine them hurrying around under all those lights, between so many tall buildings. As soon as I thought about them, my belly warmed at the memory of the night before. Were they thinking about it this morning, too?

A delicious shiver went through me when I remembered the way Waylon had just thrown me down on the table and devoured me. Picturing it made me wet, my body heating up in anticipation of it happening again. I couldn't wait to feel his tongue inside me ...Sawyer's playful lips on my skin...Holden's simple words that made me feel so very naughty.

If Charlie liked bad girls, well, he'd love me now.

I snuggled into my parka with a smug smile at the thought of him coming over to Haley's after I caught him cheating. Begging for me to hear him out while I pelted his car with eggs. To my surprise, the memory no longer tore into my heart like barbed wire through skin. Maybe what they said was true. The best way to get over a guy was to get under another.

And I'd sure done that. Well, I still hadn't technically had sex, but I was calling that a technicality. Waylon had all the way fucked me the night before. There was no other way to describe the way his tongue had plunged into me, opening me and claiming me. Picturing it had me squirming in the saddle, tightening my knees against the horse. Van Gogh must have taken that as an urge to go faster, because she began to canter smoothly along the trail.

The motion did not help my situation. As she rocked under me, I began to move with the rhythm. Okay, now I knew why women in the old days had to ride side-saddle. If I scooched forward just a little bit, the saddle horn rubbed right against my swollen, needy clit. Enjoying the sensation, I scooted forward a bit more, holding onto the saddle horn with one hand and rocking against it. I pictured Sawyer's cock as he'd stroked it the night before. Instead of a saddle horn, I was grinding against Sawyer's shaft.

I gripped the head of it, rocking faster, picturing his strong hands around my hips, helping me along.

Unfortunately, his strong hands were not there to steady me when Van Gogh veered as she slipped on the snow. My foot swung free of the stirrup, but Van Gogh quickly regained her stride. My foot flailed for the stirrup, but in my awkward position, too far forwards on the saddle, I couldn't get it. Dropping the reigns, I threw my arms around her neck, clinging on for dear life. As I stretched my leg towards the stirrup, I suddenly slipped towards that side. I tried to throw my balance back to center, but it was too late. One second I was on her back, and the next I was on my back.

Fuck.

I'd just tried to masturbate while riding a

horse. There was something seriously wrong with me.

Something called *need-to-get-laid-itis*.

Now I was a mile from the house, lying in a foot of snow, while Van Gogh was probably well on her way home. Or hell, she had probably done that on purpose and was now skipping about like the sassy wench she was, glad to be free.

At least the snow had cushioned my fall. I pushed myself up, only to see one of the side-by-sides puttering along the trail from the other direction. Well, this was just craptastic. One of the guys had yet again witnessed me looking like a complete idiot. But hey, it was their fault. If it was Sawyer, I might even tell him why I'd fallen.

As the cart drew closer, I stood and brushed snow off my butt with the thick gloves Holden had gotten me in town. When I turned back, the side-by-side was bumping along the trail, almost on me.

My heart sank. It wasn't one of the guys. Mr. Grimes was coming to my rescue.

SEVENTEEN

Amber

Suddenly, having one of my stepbrothers see my latest farm folly seemed like a wonderful option. Definitely preferable to creepy Mr. Grimes.

"That was some kind of acrobatics," he said as the cart rocked to a halt.

"Yeah, I guess I'm not the best rider yet," I said.

"You were awfully far forward in the saddle," he said, studying my face with narrowed eyes.

"Was I?" I asked innocently, trying to keep the heat of my indignation from rising to my face.

Had the creep been watching me? Oh my God, did he know what I'd been doing? Had he seen me squirming around, rubbing against the saddle horn?

I wanted to die.

"I'll tell you what," Mr. Grimes said after a minute. "I'll give you a ride home if you hop up in

108

here and give me some of what you been giving those brothers of yours."

"Excuse me?"

"I know what you city girls are like," he said. "A different dick every night of the week. Now you come out here, probably got yourself a necklace with keys to each of your brother's bedrooms. At least I'm not kin to you."

My mouth dropped open as he unzipped his canvas coveralls.

"If that pussy's not too good to share with your own brothers, it's not too good to share with me," he said. "What's one more dick going to matter at this point?"

He pulled out his wrinkly old cock and gave it a good stroke. I tried not to gag as it flopped about, half erect.

"I know why you're here," Grimes said. "My wife says you got in trouble back in New York. Got knocked up, did you? Don't worry, I've been snipped. You can ride this stallion bareback."

Stallion? I might have laughed out loud if I wasn't so horrified. I mean, I'd been flashed on the sidewalk in New York before, but it wasn't like I stuck around to see those scrawny dicks struggling to get hard in twenty-degree weather.

"What the hell is wrong with you?" I screeched, at last finding my voice. "You're propositioning me in the same sentence as you're talking about your wife?"

"Don't pretend you got morals," he said. "Not when you're letting your brothers diddle you every night. Besides, the wife's all worn out like an old sock. Now hop up in here and let me get my dick in that pussy while it's still young and fresh."

This was why I carried pepper spray in my purse.

But I didn't carry it out here. There were exactly four men in a ten mile radius from me, and I wanted three of them. I didn't figure I'd need it. But of course it would be that fourth guy who would remind me why I carried protection in the first place.

Since I didn't have any, I bent over, grabbed a giant handful of snow, and hurled it into his lap, right on his scrawny little pencil dick.

"You can take your little golf cart and stick it up your side-by-side ass," I said.

Good one, Amber. What does that even mean?

But apparently, it didn't have to make sense. He got the message. He started beating snow off his dick and howling curses at me. "You're going to regret this, you dirty whore," he bellowed.

"I seriously doubt that," I said. But because I was basically defenseless, I thought it might be wise to remind him that the Westling brothers had my back. "And if you try to make trouble, I'll tell the guys what you said to me."

"You're nothing but a worthless cock-tease," he said, shoving himself back into his coveralls. "I didn't say anything you didn't invite. You're a cheap slut, spreading your legs for every man on the ranch, and then having the nerve to act surprised when a man gets in line for his turn."

"You don't know anything about me," I said, my hands balling into fists. For a horrible moment, I thought I might cry. What if that's how it looked to everyone else? Haley's words echoed in my mind. Everyone who found out would have this reaction. I'd be the filthy whore who let her stepbrothers pass her around to get their rocks off.

Then an even worse thought entered my mind. What if the guys saw it that way, too? That I was just something to share, a good fuck followed by high-fives all around?

"I know one thing about you," Grimes said. "If you know what's good for you and those brothers of yours, you'll keep your mouth shut about this. I'd hate to see them lose the ranch over a lousy piece of ass. You're probably so loose I'd be rattling around in there like a pencil in a tin can."

"You got the pencil part right," I shot back.

"Enjoy your walk," he said with a nasty smile, and he shifted into gear and drove off, leaving me fuming in the snow.

I was so pissed I thought my head would explode. I kicked savagely at the snow, sending sprays of it up into the sunlight, where it fell, glittering like...well, glitter. After a minute, my fury had receded, and I stopped kicking and took a breath, wiping snow off my pants and turning back towards the house. I couldn't even see it from here.

Trying to keep the cold from seeping through my boots into my feet, I wiped off the toes of my riding boots. It didn't matter much, though. I wasn't wearing snow boots, or ski boots, or even Uggs. I was wearing leather riding boots, and my toes were like ice within a minute. Stomping towards the house, I began to fume all over again.

Stupid Grimes. Stupid Van Gogh. Stupid brothers for making me so sexually frustrated I'd tried to get off on a moving horse. Stupid Mom for sending me out here. Stupid Charlie for never wanting to have sex with me but letting some random ginger ride his face. Stupid Senator Westling for marrying my mother in Africa and thinking it was a good idea to tell me on the same night they told the rest of the political world.

By the time I made it back to the house, I was thoroughly frozen and twice as pissed as when I'd started walking.

I barged into the house and straight to the kitchen, where the wood stove was crackling. Sawyer was at the cook stove, frying bacon.

"Where you been?" he asked. "You look cold."

"I am cold," I growled, ripping off my gloves and tossing them on the table. "I just walked about a mile in the snow."

"What'd you do that for?" he asked, barely glancing at me.

"Because your douche-nozzle farmhand wouldn't give me a ride unless I agree to have sex with him."

So much for not telling the guys. I was way too pissed to play that game.

That got Sawyer's attention, though. He turned from the stove, a fork in one hand, his face weirdly devoid of emotion. "What did you say?"

I gulped. Maybe opening my mouth had been a huge mistake, like Grimes had warned. The guys were so loyal, and for all I knew, Grimes had been living there since their grandfather owned the ranch.

"Um, I didn't, obviously," I said.

"But he asked you to?"

"I'm not sure if he actually asked," I said.

"Go ring the dinner bell for me," he said, turning back to the stove.

My eyes stung. That was it? So as long as Grimes had politely asked me to hop on his shriveled old penis, it was okay?

Swallowing hard, I headed out back to ring the bell. What else could I do? It wasn't like Grimes had hurt me. He hadn't tried anything. He'd just showed me his dick, and it wasn't like I'd never seen one of those before.

I rang the bell and trudged back inside, hung up my jacket, and started up the stairs.

"Can you come in here a minute, Amber?" Sawyer asked.

I readied myself for the worst and stepped

back into the kitchen. "What's up?" I asked, suddenly feeling awkward in the house I'd gotten so used to that I thought of it as home now.

"I want you to tell us exactly what happened," he said. "When we're all here."

Holden came in, stomping off his boots by the door before entering the kitchen. My heart started hammering as we waited for Waylon. I never knew how he'd react.

When at last he showed up, my hands were thawed and I was warming my toes next to the wood stove. Sawyer had set four plates of BLTs on the table, and I slid into a chair, dreading this moment. On the walk back, I'd imagined telling them and then going out to tell off that pervert. But now that I had to say those things out loud, I didn't want to. I didn't want the guys to know that anyone saw me that way, even an old perv like Grimes.

"Grimes needs to go," Sawyer said before I could speak.

"What?" I squeaked.

Waylon frowned and picked up his sandwich.

"What happened?" Holden asked.

"He crossed the line," Sawyer said. "With Amber."

Three sets of eyes fixed on me. Sawyer's usually playful blue eyes were steady and fierce. Holden's warm brown eyes were reassuring and concerned. Waylon's dark eyes were stormy and...a bit frightening. I gulped and set down my sandwich without taking a bite.

"What did he do?" Waylon asked, his voice flat.

"He didn't do anything," I said. "Well, I mean, he didn't do anything to me. He just whipped out his dick and kind of...told me to...you know. Sit on it. Or, I think the word he used was *ride*."

Holden's eyes bulged, and he reached out to take my hand. "Are you okay?"

"I'm fine," I said. "He told me not to tell you or we'd all be sorry, so I probably shouldn't have, but—."

"You should have," Waylon said.

"I should have told you, or I should have...?"

"Told us," he growled. "You're one of us now. What happens to one of us, happens to all of us."

"If that's the case, then next time I'd appreciate it if I wasn't the one who actually had to see the disgusting little grub."

Waylon stood, his chair legs scraping the floor. "There won't be a next time," he said.

Without a word, the other two stood, picked up their hats, and followed him out. I ran out on the porch after them before I remembered I'd taken off my boots to warm my feet. "Don't kill him," I begged, grabbing Holden's arm.

"Go back inside," he said, his voice gentle but firm. "We'll be back soon."

What had they said about cowboy justice? I

definitely should have kept my mouth shut. Probably. Surely they wouldn't really kill him. I mean, this wasn't the wild west. But the way they strode off towards the barn, not in a crazy way like they were going to beat the shit out of him but in a purposeful way, made me cold all the way to my toes.

Not that my poor toes needed another reason to be cold. The pain of standing on the frozen porch got the better of me, and I ran back inside. I started to put on my boots, but then I realized that whatever cowboy justice involved, I didn't want to see it. I'd already been arrested once this year, and I didn't want to be an accomplice in someone's murder, or a witness in his castration, or have anything else to do with Grimes—ever. I'd seen more than enough of him to last a lifetime.

So I slumped down on the couch and called Haley.

EIGHTEEN

Amber

"I saw my first real-life penis," I told Haley a few minutes later, after she'd told me about the community service her mom was making her do.

"Oooh, which one?" she asked.

"Two, actually," I said. "One was not impressive."

"Aww," she said, laughing. "Did one of the brothers get the short end of the dick? I mean, stick?"

"It's not one of the brothers," I said. And then for the second time that day, I recounted events with Grimes.

"Oh my God, that's so gross," she squealed, which made me feel totally validated. I started to relax.

"It really was," I said. "I'm glad I saw Sawyer's yesterday or that would have been my first mental dick pic."

"No, there was that guy who flashed us

outside the pizza place," she said.

"Oh, and that one in Central Park when we were kids."

"Oh, God, I forgot about him," she agreed. "But then, I have a brother who ran around with no pants until he was, like, ten."

"Eww," I said. "Actually, I guess I saw Mark's, too. Does it count if I don't remember?"

"Definitely not," she said decisively. "So, are you going to tell me all about Sawyer's penis, or am I going to have to come out there and see it for myself?"

Before I could answer, Holden came back in, stomped the snow off his boots, and took off his hat. I told Haley I'd call her later, since I didn't really want to describe Sawyer's cock with his brother in the room. I still wasn't sure how much they were okay with sharing.

"What happened?" I asked Holden when I'd hung up.

Holden shrugged. "My brothers will take care of him."

"What does that mean?" I asked, jumping up and going to the window. I couldn't see anyone out there.

"He'll be fine," Holden said, taking my shoulder and turning me towards him.

"Are you sure?"

"I'm sure." He looked me straight in the eye, and I relaxed a little. Holden wouldn't lie to me. He towered over me, and yet, I felt nothing but safe with him there. When a car started outside, he pulled me close and wrapped his arms around me. I rested my head against his wide, strong chest. "What about you?" he murmured. "Are you okay?"

"Yeah, just grossed out," I said. "And I really didn't want anything to happen to him. I mean, I was pissed, but it wasn't a big deal."

"It is a big deal," he said quietly. "No one disrespects our girl like that."

I felt a swell of warmth inside, and I snuggled closer to his chest. I was their girl.

*

Holden stayed with me for an hour, holding me in front of the fire until the door swung open and the others stomped in. Sawyer hung up his coat and came to warm himself by the fire with us.

"Well?" I asked. "What happened?"

"He won't be bothering you again," Waylon said flatly.

"Did you..." I broke off and gulped, not sure I wanted to know the answer to the next question. "Is he still alive?"

"If he'd laid a finger on you, he wouldn't be," Waylon said. He shoved his hat lower on his head and glowered at the fire. "It's going to be tough around here without him."

"What are you saying?" I asked. "It's not my fault you kicked his ass. I didn't ask you to do that."

"And no one is blaming you," Holden assured

me, squeezing my shoulders.

"He got what was coming to him," Sawyer said. "I just don't know how we're going to replace him. Not this winter, that's for sure."

"I don't know if he can be replaced," Holden said quietly. "He runs this ranch as much as the three of us."

"We'll just have to make do," Waylon said.

And even though they said it wasn't my fault, it sure felt like it. I sat up straighter, grateful for Holden's strong body beside mine. "I'll take over the rest of the chores with the horses," I said. "I feed and exercise them every day, but I can muck out the stalls and put their bedding down, too."

"You don't have to do all that," Holden said.

"I'm not a vet, and I can't put shoes on them or anything, but I can take over their general care," I said. "And I can do the recordkeeping and accounting stuff for the whole ranch. I'm getting bored with decorating, anyway."

The guys looked around the room, taking in the new throw pillows on the couch, the decorative gourds on the coffee table, the candles on the end tables and the mantle, the wreathes hanging on either side of the fireplace.

"It looks nice," Sawyer said.

"Yeah, like a home," I said. "But seriously, let me help. Even if it's not my fault that Grimes is gone. If I'm part of this family now, if I'm going to be part of your lives, really let me in. Not as a guest, but as an equal, who does her fair share just like the three of you."

"Don't worry, you'll have plenty to keep you busy at night," Sawyer said. "It's going to be a lot of work taking care of the needs of three men. We need you well rested."

"She's not a sex slave," Waylon growled. "If she wants to work, she can work."

"Thank you," I said, shooting him a grateful look. I was surprised he'd step in on my behalf. If anything, I thought he'd be the one who insisted I have nothing to do with the ranch business. He was so private about everything else, I didn't feel like I knew him at all yet.

You know what his tongue feels like inside you, a little voice reminded me. Excitement blossomed in my belly at the thought. Would they want to taste me again tonight?

"We haven't had a good bookkeeper in a while," Sawyer said. "Not since…"

"Maria?" I asked.

"I'm going to work on my car," Waylon said, pushing his hat lower and stomping out.

"Okay, then," I said. "I guess I hit the nail on the head there."

"Not Maria," Sawyer said.

"Ah," I said, nodding. "Your brother, then."

Holden nodded. "Waylon took it hardest."

I was pretty sure they'd all taken it hard, but it had been Waylon's fiancé. At first, I'd thought he had no feelings to hurt, but now I knew why he'd built those walls around his heart. My heart went out to him. I knew what it felt like to be cheated on, discarded for someone else. I knew how that betrayal felt, and it was bad enough when I'd gone through it. I couldn't imagine how much it would hurt if the girl he betrayed me with had been Haley, the closest thing I had to a sister. I probably would have died.

I stood and plucked my jacket from a peg near the door. "I'll go talk to him."

NINETEEN

Amber

I was halfway to the shop when a disheveled, wheezing, red-faced Mrs. Grimes came rushing to intercept me. I froze in midstride. Somehow, I'd forgotten about her. But of course the guys hadn't roughed up an old woman and left her in a ditch somewhere. Which was a tiny bit unfortunate, because she looked like she was about to rough me up. I had no idea how to fight, let alone how to fend off cowgirl justice.

"You little hussy," Mrs. Grimes huffed. "I know what you did, and you're going to pay for it."

I held up both hands. "Um, please don't hit me?"

"You deserve everything you've got coming to you," she snarled, her round face contorted into an ugly mask of hatred. "Trying to seduce a godly, married man!"

"What?" I asked, dropping my hands. "What

are you talking about?"

"You know what I'm talking about," she said. "As if spreading your legs for your own stepbrothers wasn't enough, you had to go after a hardworking, honest man like my husband? And to get him fired when he refused you! You should be ashamed of yourself."

"Whoa, whoa, whoa," I said. "Look here, I don't know what your husband told you, but I definitely did not go after him. Not that there's anything wrong with your husband, I'm sure he's great and all, but not my type."

"Oh, now you're dragging his name through the mud? You think you're all that, with your young little body and that swishy hair of yours. But my husband is above temptation from harlots like you."

"I'm sure he is," I said, edging towards the shop, hoping Waylon would step out and come to my rescue. But it looked like this time, I was on my own.

"You may not know a lick about morals, so let me tell you this," Mrs. Grimes went on, stalking closer and closer as she spoke. "My husband is an upstanding citizen of this community. He would rather lose his job than compromise his reputation. Unfortunately, I can't say the same for the men of that house." She nodded towards the lodge, which was painfully silent.

"No one is doing anything to damage their reputation," I said.

"Oh, save me the excuses." She stuck her

pointy little index finger right in my face. "No one will believe the lies of a slut like you when this comes out. And mark my words, it will come to light. You can't keep filth like this hidden forever."

"As nice as it's been talking to you, I'm just going to go on and take care of the horses," I said, edging towards the barn.

"You'll burn in hell for this day," she said, her eyes flashing with sick gleefulness. "The devil will ram his fiery pitchfork right up that flapping flytrap and fry you over the flames of hell like a piece of meat on a spit." She thrust an imaginary pitchfork at me, and I jumped back with a yelp, slipping on the snow. Mrs. Grimes used my imbalance to her advantage, giving me a hard shove.

I pinwheeled my arms, flailing for a second before falling flat on my ass. Okay, that was it. I'd played nice, been a good, diplomatic senator's daughter. But I wasn't going to be pushed around by this old bat. I leapt to my feet and pushed Mrs. Grimes's shoulder. She rocked back and then forward, trying to get her own balance on the slippery snow.

Instead of falling, she pitched forwards, grabbing my arms with both hands. We circled, each trying to wrestle the other's feet out from under the other.

"You kiss your mother with that mouth?" I asked, trying to knock her sideways.

"You want to talk about mothers?" she asked,

stomping on my foot as we continued gripping each other's arms like we were caught up in a demented dance. "What will your mother have to say when she finds out you've been diddling your own brothers?"

"Stepbrothers," I growled, yanking my foot from under hers and kicking out at her shin.

"I'm sure she'll be happy to find out exactly what you're out here doing," she said. "On your back for all three of them, I bet."

"What, are you jealous?" I asked. "You sound like you've thought this through an awful lot. Not that I blame you. A girl can have her fantasies, am I right?"

Mrs. Grimes's mouth dropped open in a giant huff, and her face turned red with rage. Or hell, maybe it was embarrassment. I mean, a girl couldn't help fantasizing about all three of the Westling boys pleasuring her at once. It was only human.

"You filthy Jezebel," she howled.

I decided to forgive her for lusting after my men and for judging me so harshly. It was probably just jealousy. After all, she was stuck with Mr. Grimes. I knew how much it sucked to find out the guy you thought was perfect was actually a cheating, other-girl's-pussy-eating piece of shit.

"I forgive you," I said.

Her eyes burned with more rage than I'd ever seen on anyone's face in my life. "What?"

"I know it sucks to love a cheater," I said. "So I forgive you for blaming me."

I thought I was being the bigger person, but obviously Mrs. Grimes did not agree. The next second, she kicked me in the shin so hard I yelped and lifted my foot. My other foot slipped, and I tumbled to the ground again. But this time, I was holding onto Mrs. Grimes. She sprawled on top of me, then flopped over, slipped and collapsed onto me again.

"Ooof," I moaned as the air shot out of my lungs.

Mrs. Grimes scrambled to her feet, trying to look all high and mighty even with her hat halfway over her eyes, snow stuck all over her coat, and her arms wobbling for balance.

"I'll make you pay for this if it's the last thing I ever do," she said, drawing up a ball of spit and hocking it right onto my face.

I screamed in disgust and hurled snow at her, flailing on the ground as I tried to grab her legs. She kicked a spray of snow into my face before she tottered off.

Sitting up, I wiped the spit off my face. I decided right then and there to start carrying pepper spray again. And maybe take a class in self-defense.

I was officially not a fan of cowgirl justice.

TWENTY

Amber

I'd almost forgotten why I was there, but once I scraped my ass up off the ground, I headed for the shop. This time, I wasn't fueled by righteous rage at my mistreatment. In fact, I kinda wanted to keep this one to myself. I wasn't exactly proud of the fact that I'd just had my ass handed to me by a doddering old lady.

Waylon was leaned up under the hood of his car, like usual.

"Did you fire Mr. Grimes?" I asked.

"What kind of question is that?" he asked, standing and fixing me with those black, unreadable eyes.

"Well, I thought you did," I said. "I just wondered what was going to happen to Mrs. Grimes."

"I got no beef with her," Waylon said, leaning back down with his wrench. "Unless you do."

"No," I said lightly.

"You think we'd let that bastard stay here after what he said to you?" Waylon growled.

"No, I was just wondering about her," I said. "You think she'll want to stay on? I mean, you did just beat up her husband. At least, I assume that's what you did. Not that I know. I wasn't following you and spying or anything. You can ask Holden. I was with him the whole time. I just figured since he's not working here, he wouldn't be living here, and Mrs. Grimes—."

Waylon stood abruptly, fixing me with his intense gaze.

My words cut off mid-thought, and I gulped down more of them. "Sorry."

"Whatever Mrs. Grimes wants to do, she's welcome to do," he said. "As long as she's not fucking with us or what's ours."

Did that mean me? The thought gave me another thrill of excitement and pride. I was theirs. And they were mine.

"And if she is?" I asked. I didn't want to tell him she'd slapped me around, since I hated the thought of them beating up an old lady. Not that they'd do that. Right? Surely Wyoming justice took into account a person's gender.

"Is she?" he asked.

"No, but hypothetically, what if she was?"

"Let's worry about that when the time comes," he said, studying me intently. "We got plenty to worry about already."

"Like the ranch?"

Waylon's back stiffened. "Like the ranch," he agreed.

"What if you sold, like, a little piece of it?" I asked. "Could you get enough from the sale to save the rest?"

"We're not selling the ranch," he said, his hands curling around the edge of the engine well.

"I just meant a little piece."

He glared death rays at me. "No."

"Okay," I said, holding up my hands. "I was just trying to help."

"A bookkeeper who wants to sell the ranch," he growled in disgust, then twisted savagely on something in the engine. A curl of fire licked to life inside me. Damn, he was sexy, even when he was pissed. Maybe especially then. I imagined that bolt was my nipple he was twisting, and my knees quaked.

I shook my head, clearing away the nighttime thoughts. Today, we had business to attend to. And I was determined to be a professional if I worked here, just like they were. If such a thing as professional ranchers existed. They took it seriously, going out before dawn every morning and working until dark most days. If I was going to play my part, I was going to work just as hard.

But with a few more hours of sleep.

I'd known he wouldn't go for selling part of the ranch. That's why I had put that idea in his head first. Now I could revisit my real dream.

"What about renting out the cabins?" I asked, then rushed ahead before he could shoot me down. "Mrs. Grimes can clean them after guests, or I will, if she leaves. I'll decorate them with an authentic cowboy vibe so guests can feel like they're being all rugged and rustic, but they'll be staying in comfy cabins."

Waylon grunted. I stepped up and put a hand on his sculpted bicep.

"I'm sure you've seen going by on their way to the Tetons. Imagine letting them stay here, holed up in a warm cabin while having ready access to the mountains. It'll be cheaper than up in Jackson Hole, but close enough to get back after skiing and stay the night. And we could offer horseback riding lessons. Holden's an excellent teacher, as I can attest to myself."

"I'll think about it," Waylon muttered.

"Really?" I'd expected to have to work on him a little more, wear him down. At first, I was thrilled. But a chill went through me, too. How bad must it be that he was agreeing so readily? I supposed I would see when I started doing the bookkeeping. I had a feeling it wouldn't be good.

TWENTY-ONE

Amber

A few nights later at dinner, Holden served us all beef stew before sitting down to join us. It was the perfect meal for a cold winter's night, and for once, the wind had fallen silent outside.

We were in the middle of dinner when Sawyer's phone rang in his pocket. For a second, the guys all froze, which made me freeze. Were girls still calling them, and if so, why didn't they just answer and tell the other girls to bug off? This wasn't the first time someone had called while I was there and they didn't answer.

Did they have that many girls on reserve for cold winter nights like this?

"You gonna answer that?" I asked, trying to keep my voice light.

"Nah, it's not important," Sawyer said, offering me a smile that for once didn't reach his eyes. He silenced his phone without removing it from his pocket.

"Any word on Grimes?" I asked, trying to make conversation.

"I ran into Mrs. Grimes this evening," Sawyer said. "She had some things to say."

"Is that right?" I asked, popping a piece of potato into my mouth. If they could play mysterious, so could I.

"Uh huh," he said. "I think we came to an agreement in the end."

"What's that?" I asked.

"It seems she'd be better suited for a job somewhere in town."

Okay, maybe I couldn't play mysterious. I wanted to know the whole story, and I was too freaked out by the possible repercussions of the Grimeses living in town to hide it.

I gulped and looked from one of my stepbrothers to the next. "Are we going to be okay?"

"That depends on what you call okay," Waylon said.

"Whatever happens, we'll weather it together," Holden said, leaning in to cover my hand with his. My hand completely disappeared under the massive size of his. Damn, I wanted those hands. All over my body. Every night.

"Do you think she'll start shit in town?" I asked.

"No telling," Sawyer said. "But we should be ready for it if she does."

"Ready for the world to think I'm a total whore," I said, laughing a little. It was only funny because I was still a freaking virgin, but somehow, I was also the world's biggest slut. I only wished I had the credentials to live up to that name.

"We'll be here for you, no matter what happens," Waylon said. "That's a promise."

"It won't change the way we feel about you," Sawyer said, reaching over to slide his hand under mine. His fingers laced through mine, Holden's hand still covering them.

"And you're not a whore," Holden said, squeezing my hand. "You're perfect."

"I don't know about perfect," I said. "But I'll work on the whore part."

They all looked at me blankly for a second. But hey, If I was going to be labeled a whore, I might as well make the most of it, right?

Whatever happened, whatever people said about me, it would be worth it if I got to be with any one of them. And I didn't have to choose just one. I could have all three of them. I couldn't wait to see just how good it would be.

"Well," I said at last. "If they're going to talk, let's give them something to talk about."

A Note From the Author

Thank you for reading *Wrangle Me, Cowboys*. If you enjoy reading about Amber and her cowboys, make sure to leave a review. A couple lines is all it takes, and I'd be so happy to hear your thoughts!

Keep reading for a short excerpt of book 3 or find the complete Book 3 on Amazon.

Excerpt of Book 3

Ride Me, Cowboys
By Alexa B. James

Amber

As I rode Van Gogh back into the yard after an afternoon ride, I spotted a U-Haul truck in front of the Grimes's cabin, and a wave of relief and excitement went through me. Relief because the creepy Mr. Grimes and his holier-than-thou wife were leaving. Excitement because that meant the five cabins behind the lodge where I was living in sin with my three sinfully sexy stepbrothers would be empty.

After more than a month of resisting the idea of renting the cabins to tourists, Waylon had given in. Which meant I had a new project, and if there was one thing I loved, it was a project. Which might have had a tiny bit to do with the fact that I was a bit of a project myself.

I swung down off Van Gogh, feeling quite pleased with how much I'd progressed in my riding technique. I'd just dismounted with the poise of a real cowgirl. I strutted towards the barn, leading the beautiful white horse towards his stall. Now that

Grimes had been fired for being a giant dick to me—or puny dick, to be precise—I had my hands full taking care of the four horses on the ranch.

After I'd brushed down Van Gogh and put up his saddle and gear, I turned just in time to see Mrs. Grimes coming around the corner of the barn.

Shit. Just who I didn't want to see. I'd already seen way too much of her when she told me off for getting her husband fired. I could only imagine the earful I was about to get now that she'd been fired, too.

But hey, it wasn't my fault she attacked me and called me a whore. Okay, maybe the whore part was my fault. But what was a girl to do when every one of her stepbrothers was hotter than the last...and willing to share?

I spotted the ladder leading up to the hay loft and decided to go for it. It looked a little rickety, and I'd never used it before. But if crotchety old Mr. Grimes could get up and down it, surely I could. It would save my pride, and my backside, from another run-in with the old witch. With a glance over my shoulder, I started up the ladder.

"First she gets me fired and now she runs like a coward instead of facing me," Mrs. Grimes behind me.

Craptastic. She'd seen me.

"Maybe I'd prefer not to get thrown in the snow again," I said, turning halfway around. I clung to the ladder and looked down at Mrs. Grimes.

"Oh, don't pretend that hurt," she huffed, her eyes glittering with malice as she scurried over to the ladder.

My mouth dropped open when she grabbed the rungs of the wooden ladder. It might hold me, but there was no way it was going to hold two of us. It was already shaking and swaying with my every step.

"Don't climb up," I yelled, my hand shooting out, as if I could stop her from halfway up. "We'll both fall."

"Then get your scrawny ass down here and tell me to my face how you didn't mean to come in here conniving to get me and my husband both fired."

"I didn't," I protested, hugging the ladder as she shook it. It swayed and creaked alarmingly.

"Get down here, you little hussy," she barked, shaking the ladder harder. "Or I'll come up there and get you myself."

I looked down, and then up at the dozen steps left before the loft.

"I'd like to see you try, you big hussy," I exploded, fear taking over and activating my no-filter mode. Making a snap decision, I scampered up the rungs as fast as I could. The ladder scraped sideways as I reached the last few steps. Mrs. Grimes screeched in fury below, but I didn't stop to see if she was climbing up or just trying to knock me off.

It had to be at least twenty feet to the floor, and I wasn't keen on breaking my neck. The nearest hospital was probably hours away from Coyote Ranch.

I grabbed the edge of the loft as the ladder began to tip, moving slowly to one side. With a shriek of fear, I hauled myself up, my legs kicking at empty air as I dove headfirst into a pile of straw. My heart slammed in my chest, my legs shaking with adrenaline. If I was going to die young, I did *not* want my cause of death to be listed as "an accident in a barn." I may have been adjusting to ranch life, but I wasn't that country yet.

"You can run, but you can't hide!" Mrs. Grimes squawked from below.

I hung my head over the edge of the loft to see her panting and straining to lift the ladder, which has slid over against one wall. If she was trying to straighten it, that meant she was going to climb it. And from the look on her face, she wasn't above tossing me from the hayloft and pretending it was an accident.

Who would people believe, the cherry-cheeked cheerful old lady or the New York party girl? She'd probably say I was drunk and had fallen out myself.

Determined not to let her reach me, I crawled along the loft to where the platform met the wall. The ladder was propped in the corner between the two, so I grabbed the top rungs and braced myself to push it away from the wall. Mrs. Grimes must have seen my intention, because she jerked at the ladder from below. Nearly toppling off, I let go of the ladder, which smacked back into the corner with a splintering crack. Whoever won control of the ladder, it didn't look like either of us would be using it. Not without risk of it collapsing into a pile of boards and nails.

"Leave me alone," I yelled down.

"I don't think so," she yelled back, yanking at the ladder.

I grabbed the top, pulled it back, and shoved as hard as I could. It tottered for a moment before tipping. It started slow, but as it gained momentum, it began to move faster. Mrs. Grimes's eyes widened, and she backpedaled to get clear of it as it crashed to the floor with a giant whoosh, sending up a cloud of dust. The horses neighed and danced nervously in their stalls.

"You tried to kill me," Mrs. Grimes screeched.

"Um, hello, you tried to knock me off a ladder," I shouted back.

"That's it," she yelled. "I've had it with you and all these disgusting men. I'm calling the law on you." With that, she whirled around and marched out of the barn.

I jumped up, ready to run and tell the guys. Only then did I realize that once again, I'd gotten myself royally stuck.

2

Amber

I didn't want the guys to have to come back in from working to get me, so I settled down in the hay to wait. I was wearing nice warm clothes from my ride, and the day was sunny and warmer than usual, probably above freezing for once. Once Mrs. Grimes left, and I knew she wasn't going to climb up and get me, it was kind of nice up there. When I heard the U-Haul pull out of the driveway, and I started to relax. The smell of the hay reminded me of the guys, and I snuggled down into it, thinking about them.

The next thing I knew, I was waking up from a delicious dream of all three men devouring me, to the sound of voices outside the barn. I crawled to the edge of the loft and yelled as loud as I could, and the voices stopped. I sat down on the hay and pulled out my phone. Now that I had all their numbers, I wasn't sure which guy to text. Waylon had already rescued me one too many times, and I didn't want him thinking I was more of a dumbass than he already did. On the other hand, I didn't want the others thinking I was a dumbass at all.

In the end, the barn door opened, so I just called out to Sawyer, who had walked through the door, looking more gorgeous than ever with his felt cowboy hat pulled down over his blonde hair. I waved wildly from the loft, calling down until he looked up. He just shook his head and started picking up the ladder.

"Be careful," I called. "It might be broken."

A minute later, his smiling face appeared over the edge of the loft. "What are you doing up here?" he asked.

"Oh, thank you, baby Jesus," I said.

"Well, I'm not baby Jesus, but you can thank me any time, Princess."

"I intend to," I said, my dream still fresh in my mind.

"Is that right?"

"That's one hundred percent correct."

"Then let's have it," he said climbing the last few rungs of the ladder and hopping up into the loft.

"Right now?" I squeaked, looking up at him. His hair had grown out a little, so it curled at the back of his neck, peeking out from under his hat. The sun slanted in the windows, and tiny hairs on his arms gleamed, outlining his shape in the sunlight.

He grinned down at me, a challenge in his eyes. "No time like the present."

"Okay," I said with a gulp. "But I've never done this before. I mean, I've watched it done. Not in person—well, not unless you count when I walked in on my boyfriend and another girl, but let's not get into that. What I mean is, I've learned what I could from watching, you know, educational videos, so I might not totally suck. I mean, I'll suck, but in a good way, at least I hope so."

Sawyer cocked an eyebrow, smirking at my verbal tirade. "You mean you watched porn."

"For educational purposes only," I protested.

He grinned and nodded, his eyes flicking from my face down toward his zipper. I eased forward, then knelt up and ran my hands up the back of his legs. His calves were hard, his thighs even harder. My breath came faster as I looked up at his face. His smile remained, but his eyes were fierce with desire. I trembled at the intensity of his gaze. Biting my lip, I slid my hands around his thighs, pushing my fingers between them.

He reached down, stroking the back of my head, then running his hand around my jaw, lifting my chin. His thumb stroked my lower lip, pulling my lips apart. "You don't have to thank me this way if you don't want," he said, his voice slightly hoarse.

"Oh, I want." If I'd been uncertain before, his offer to let me off the hook sealed it. I wiggled my fingers, then drew my hands up further, over his firm ass, and tugged him until he took one step closer. The fly of his jeans was inches from my face. I felt like a kid on Christmas morning as I unbuttoned his jeans. I was going to touch my very first in-the-flesh penis, and I could not wait.

*

To read the completed book 3, search for Alexa B. James on Amazon today!